"They'll not get you!"

"Ma, I don't want anyone killed because of me," Elisabeth protested, anxiously rubbing her forehead, trying to think. "Maybe I should go."

"No! You're not that squaw's daughter. And they'll keep you once they get you into their camp. I've heard the miners and trappers talking. The Indians want white women." She paused to catch her breath. "You were kidnapped from another wagon train," she said forcefully, her tone more rational. "We all knew that."

A fist pounded the door. "Open up, Mary," Jed yelled. "We gotta do something."

As she unbolted the door and he burst into the kitchen, a torrent of words spilled from his mouth. "Them savages may not wait until sunrise. They may get a hankerin' to come back tonight." Jed rarely wore a hat, and his thinning gray hair now stood on end. He tugged at his nose, marbled with broken blood vessels.

"Her features ain't Indian, and her skin ain't real dark, but her hair and eyes. . ." He was muttering his thoughts aloud, distressing Mary even more.

Her hands clutched and unclutched the folds of her apron. "It's the craziest thing I ever heard, Jed. Elisabeth, an Indian."

PEGGY DARTY is the popular, award-winning author of novels and magazine articles who also has extensive background in television and film. Darty, who makes her home in Alabama, writes another western romance that is sure to please her many fans.

Books by Peggy Darty

HEARTSONG PRESENTS
HP143—Morning Mountain

Song
of the Dove

Peggy Darty

Heartsong Presents

A note from the Author:
I love to hear from my readers! You may write to me at the following address:

Peggy Darty
Author Relations
P.O. Box 719
Uhrichsville, OH 44683

ISBN 1-57748-061-9

SONG OF THE DOVE

Cover illustration by Randy Hamlin.

PRINTED IN THE U.S.A.

prologue

Morning Dove crept through the inky darkness to the tall red rocks and gazed into the valley below. The smoldering embers of a campfire gave a feeble glow to the circle of wagons. As Morning Dove's dark eyes moved over the sleeping camp, she thought of the palefaces and the evil spirit they had brought upon Ute land. Her dark eyes burned with anger.

Her anger was quickly tempered, however, by the gentle breath of the sleeping baby in her arms. Slowly, her eyes dropped to the child, and she lifted the rabbit skin and peered impassively into the face of the newborn girl. New fear thundered in her heart as she stared at the pale face, as pale as the moon overhead.

She had brought shame and disgrace to her people. This was not a cherished Ute whose birth would have been a joyous occasion. No warrior had brought firewood to her lodge in her final days. Nor had she gone to the birthing lodge where she could kneel on a straw-covered mat for the birth. Instead, she had fled to a secret cave when the ravaging pains began. She had begged the Great Spirit for death, but death had not come; instead, she had given birth to a healthy baby. Afterwards, she had hobbled to the icy mountain stream to bathe herself and the baby; then she had wrapped her in a rabbit skin and crept to the high red rocks. She had intended to offer the baby to the Great Spirit to purge her sin, but when she reached the jagged rocks, she had spotted the wagons in the valley, which sparked a new thought in her mind.

As she stood gazing at the settlers' wagons, Morning Dove's mind drifted back to happier days when the Utes had roamed the land freely, from the bubbling springs to the open plains. But then the palefaces had come, over Ute trails and across Ute valleys, their greedy eyes seeking the buffalo and the beaver, their careless axes felling the big cottonwoods for reckless fires that blazed high in the night skies.

Tears filled her dark eyes as she recalled the evil man—the strong, fair-skinned man with his hairy face and eyes the color of the forest pine. Her search for pinion nuts had led her into their camp, and too late, she had remembered the warning of her brother, Lone Eagle, who had cared for her since the death of their parents in the Winter of No Sun.

The man who rode the white magic dog had motioned to her, holding out a shiny wristband of silver. He had dropped down from the magic dog, speaking in a strange tongue. Curiosity chased the fear from Morning Dove's brain. Her moccasined feet stilled as he approached. Then his green eyes changed, his lips turned downward. She sensed danger, and she turned to run. But it was too late. . . .

A deep, wrenching sigh shook her now as she stared at the wagons. She suddenly knew what she must do. She would return the baby to its people, the nation of palefaces. But life would not be easy for the child—she was neither Ute nor paleface. Morning Dove's eyes lifted to the sky, again seeking guidance from the Great Spirit. She prayed for the baby girl's life, that somehow she might survive in the strange world to which she was going. The little squaw must have a spirit that would sing even when it suffered. Like her own spirit, like the name she had been given: Morning Dove. In her heart, the baby girl would always be Little Dove.

With new resolve, she began to pick her way down the rocky path leading to the valley of wagons. Soon the sun would set fire to the mountain of rocks; soon the palefaces would build their morning fires. Her steps quickened.

One wagon was swathed in darkness far from the fire and the guard. This would be the wagon she would choose for Little Dove. Her feet inched forward as drumbeats of fear pounded in her chest, and her stomach heaved as if she had drunk firewater.

Still she pushed on, moving like a wispy shadow that melted into the darkness of night as she crouched to place the baby beside the rear wheel of the wagon.

She knelt, removing the blanket from her own shoulders to make a bed for the baby. Gently, she took the tiny bundle from the rabbit skin, and she began to whimper. That was good; it was what she wanted. She pinched the tiny foot until the whimper became a stronger cry of protest. Morning Dove turned and fled through the darkness as the cry sharpened to a high thin wail.

She did not look back until she reached the high red rocks. Below her, the camp sprang to life as the small and distant cry of the baby filled the night.

She crossed her arms over her shivering shoulders and hesitated one last time to glance downward. The pale yellow flame of lanterns wavered in the darkness as loud voices drowned out the baby's cry.

As she watched the baby being lifted from the ground, Morning Dove's body began to tremble even harder in the biting cold. She had not wanted the baby who could bring evil to her village, yet her body had nourished it. And her heartbeat had quickened when she felt it *move* within her. In a strange way, she had relished the new life, and now she felt as though a piece of her soul had been torn from her and cast into the night, into the arms of the strange palefaces.

For a few more seconds, she stood as still as a spirit, watching the distant camp. . .and the sadness in her soul carved a trail of tears down her frozen cheeks.

one

Elisabeth

"Wake up, Elisabeth!"

Mary Greenwood called from the living room of a small cabin at Greenwood's Trading Post. When there was no answer, Mary wandered to the door of her daughter's bedroom and gazed with pride at the young woman sleeping peacefully in the narrow iron bed.

Sleek black hair was swept back from an oval face in one long, gleaming braid which, during her sleep, had wound itself around her slender throat. A high forehead, slim small nose, and delicate lips were balanced by prominent cheekbones over hollow cheeks.

Sunken cheeks, Mary thought, shaking her gray head. *The girl is much too thin!* As she looked at her daughter, she felt a sudden remorse for being unable to provide a better life for Elisabeth, but she'd done the best she could ever since the baby had been left at their wagon. A baby when her womb was barren!

"Wake up, Elisabeth," she repeated, speaking with a rare tenderness. Mary was usually too busy herding stray chickens, dogs, errant children, and drunken traders from her doorstep to stop for such affections, but today for some reason she lingered, gazing at her beautiful daughter. "We're still running this trading post, remember? I'm goin' on to the kitchen to build a fire. We gotta fix a bigger breakfast today. More riders came in from Taos last night."

She paused to seize a strand of steel gray hair that dared escape the fierce bun at her nape. "That Missouri family staying in the last cabin has been prowling since daybreak. The kids are probably hungry. We've got dough to knead, hoecakes to mix, and fatback to fry." Thoughts of hard work sharpened her tone. "Wake up, you hear?"

"Mmmm-hmmm." The dark head tossed on the feather pillow and one long, slender leg twitched beneath the mound of quilts.

"I'm goin'," Mary said, stomping back through the cabin and slamming the front door to underscore her command.

Mary paused on the doorstep, looking around her.

Fresh snow covered the dome of Pike's Peak, blanketed the canyons and piled up against the fence posts at their trading post. The post contained ten square, one-story buildings of slab pine with a large courtyard in the center.

Mary thrust calloused hands on her plump hips and squinted up at the sunny sky. Eighteen years of Colorado weather told her that the week's snow had ended, at least temporarily. She heaved a sigh of relief as her eyes fell to the post, scanning with pride the general store, the blacksmith shop, the guest cabins, and the kitchen-dining hall. She and her husband, Jed, had built every square inch of the place, starting from nothing. Although Jed would never admit it, his general store had drawn trappers and traders from the foothills, but it had been Mary's good cooking that kept them coming back. Now the post was the center of activity between Pueblo and Colorado City.

"I don't want to get up!" Elisabeth's voice echoed through the empty cabin as her inky lashes parted and dark eyes roamed the dim room. The thought of leaving her warm nest for another work-filled day brought a heavy sigh to her lips, yet she forced herself to toss back the covers. In her own way, she was as conscious of her duties as her mother.

She was slim and tall, with long, fine-toned legs. She made a swift leap to the small rag rug that offered a patch of warmth to her feet. Shivering into her long flannel gown, she leaned over the chest and plunged her fingers into the cold pan of water. As she splashed her sleepy face, a blur of hungry faces filled her mind. She could easily envision the crowd at breakfast, elbowing each other around the ten-foot table, grabbing food and talking with their mouths full.

She reached into the chest for her underclothes.

Fifty-niners. They had been so named for the year they started pouring into the territory. Ever since gold had been discovered at Cherry Creek, they had stampeded into the country, riding on wagon, mules, and horses. Some walked, others rode in sleek prairie schooners. Their clothes were mud-crusted, and their faces were covered with beards, but all had that same dazed look in their eyes when they talked about their diggings. "Gold fever," it was called. She shook her head, mentally scolding herself for complaining. After all, it was the miners' money that put food on their table and clothes on their backs.

Her mother's departure had admitted a gust of cold air into the small drafty cabin, and the cold quickened her movements. She yanked on her camisole and wound her long braid into a thick coil at the nape of her neck. From a peg on the wall, she lifted her gray muslin dress and tugged it over her head. The soft folds of the skirt draped over her feminine form, slid down the tiny waist and gently rounded hips, then fell to the floor, covering her only decent petticoat.

Her cold fingers moved stiffly over the buttons of

her dress as she glanced down at her shivering body, suddenly recalling those awkward years when she had been all arms and legs, as gangly as the undernourished colts in the crowded corral. Unlike her mother, most Colorado women were as thin as a blade of prairie grass as a result of their long, work-filled days. Elisabeth had finally rounded into curves at breast and hip, yet her five-foot, seven-inch body registered only a dozen or so notches over the hundred mark on the scale at the post, and her mother nagged her constantly to eat more.

She hurried into the living room, frowning at the disorder that neither she nor her mother had time to straighten. She pulled on her kid leather boots, threw her black woolen cape about her shoulders, and took a deep breath. It would be weeks before the winter broke, but to relieve the monotony, her mind seized images of the columbine that would bloom in the meadows, the crystal streams thick with trout, the golden sunshine glinting over the mountain peaks. Those images were precious treasures to her during the long harsh winters, and yet she loved Colorado.

She lifted the door latch and stepped outside, blinking into the morning sunshine. The bright light filled the depths of her dark eyes, and they gleamed like polished onyx in contrast to the pristine snow.

The creak of the gate drew her attention to the

guard who was admitting an early visitor. Her eyes widened. She had always loved horses, though she had never owned one, but now she was looking at the most beautiful horse she had ever seen. It was a black stallion, about sixteen hands high, with a white stocking extending to the left knee. Its dark coat gleamed as though oiled in the morning sunlight. After a few seconds, Elisabeth lifted her eyes from the horse to the rider. When she did, she was even more startled.

He sat tall in the saddle, wearing a fringed buckskin shirt and patched trousers. A cap of the same buckskin sat on his dark head. His face was clean shaven, and his eyes, as dark as his hair, were turned toward the general store. To her disappointment, he never once looked her way.

"Elisabeth, Elisabeth!" Tommy Ashbrowner had jumped up from his game of marbles and was racing over the snowy courtyard to her doorstep. "Are you gonna think up some kind of game for us today?"

A gentle smile touched Elisabeth's lips as she looked at Tommy, bundled to the chin in his heavy coat, yet already missing his fur hat. Pale blond curls toppled over his thin face, a face lit by a pair of twinkling blue eyes. He shifted from one foot to another, eagerly awaiting her answer.

"If I have time, Tommy." She reached out and

playfully mussed his curls. "I have a busy day and—"

"You better!" He thrust his small lips into a pout. "There ain't nothing else to do at this stinking post. Your pa won't let us have a snowball fight or do anything that's fun."

Elisabeth's smile faded as she glanced toward the general store where the tall, dark-haired man had dismounted and was quietly observing the argument in progress on the steps of the store.

Jed Greenwood, Elisabeth's adoptive father, stood haggling over a team of mules with a small, desperate-looking man. Jed was a skinny, rawboned man with thinning gray hair and an angular face.

Tommy sidled up to her. "He ain't really your pa, is he? Momma said he ain't."

The words brought a sharp ache to her heart. She had never ceased to wonder who her parents really were. Kidnapped from one wagon train and left at another by Indians, her mother had always told her. Still, she searched the faces of everyone who came to the post, wondering. . .always wondering.

"I'm sorry." The small cold hand touched hers.

Elisabeth looked down into the boy's sympathetic face, and she sighed. "He raised me, Tommy. He's the only father I've ever known. Listen," she forced a smile, "you be a good boy, and I'll try to think up a fun game for this afternoon."

"Yippee!" Tommy shouted, racing back across the courtyard to spread the news.

Watching him bound off, Elisabeth's smile faded as she pulled her hood up against the cold. Jed had never wanted her; she had always sensed that. A son would have pleased him, but he considered a girl a luxury he couldn't afford. He seemed to forget the long hours she worked in the kitchen and the time she spent entertaining the children whose parents were staying at the post until the spring thaw. But her mother always defended her, and it had been her mother's love that sustained her, providing the comfort and security she needed when she felt confused and bewildered. And she felt that way more and more as she grew older and wondered where her life was heading.

"Them mules is worth more than you're offering, Greenwood!" The little man shouted angrily.

"Take it or leave it," Jed countered, raking a hand through his tousled gray hair.

"I'd leave it." The handsome stranger who had been leaning idly against a post now took a step forward, towering over the other men. "If this man won't pay you a fair price, Ben Williamson up at Three Mile will."

Elisabeth's breath caught, and she stared in amazement. Few men challenged her father.

Jed spat a stream of tobacco juice into the snow.

"Fella, what business is it of yours?"

"I'm a missionary from the Denver area, sir. And I take offense when I see people treated unfairly. It isn't right."

"Then maybe you'd better head on back to Denver," Jed countered, "because your missionary services ain't needed here."

Elisabeth stopped walking and stared at the stranger, wondering what he would do.

"All right, sir. Good day." He unhitched his horse and climbed up in the saddle.

"Reckon I'll take that missionary's advice," the other man said with a sneer, as his eyes followed the stranger riding out of the post on his black stallion.

Elisabeth stared after the tall dark stranger for just a moment. He seemed so handsome and mysterious as he rode away, tall in the saddle. She would like to meet someone like that someday. A missionary, he had said he was. Now *that* was interesting. But she never had the chance to meet anyone interesting, and even if she did, Jed's sharp eyes were always watching her, scorning any man who was halfway friendly to her.

She turned back to the path and hurried to the one-room kitchen, lost in thought. She hated the tactics Jed used with the traders. She was secretly glad that he had failed this time. If not for the stranger, the missionary, Jed would have bought the man's mules for half their worth, fattened them cheaply, then tripled his investment when the next wagon train pulled in.

&

Glancing back toward the gate, she saw that the stranger had already disappeared. She sighed, feeling a sadness settle over her as her boots made crunching sounds in the hard-packed snow. The deep, stinging cold brought to her the familiar smells of the post—hay, leather, wood smoke. The smells of home. And yet, a part of her had never accepted the post as home, or the Greenwoods as her family. Of course she knew she was adopted; her mother had told her when she was four years old. Something more basic than that knowledge haunted her, however; it was a sense of not belonging here or anywhere, for that matter. While she had spent her life in the shadow of Pike's Peak, she had never felt at home. And yet she had tried to tell herself any girl would feel the same way, growing up at a rowdy post rather than in a civilized place like Colorado City or Denver.

The tall stranger had said he was a missionary from the Denver area. *What is Denver like?* she wondered. *And what does a missionary do?* The only missionaries she had ever known were a man and woman from Denver who had stayed at the post two years ago.

Reaching the kitchen door, she scraped her boots on the step and tried to dismiss the man from her thoughts. Considering the way Jed had behaved, she was certain she would never see the man and his beautiful horse again.

two

"It's about time!" Mary glanced at her.

"I'll catch up." Elisabeth removed her cape and dropped it on a peg by the door. She was never intimidated by her mother's strong voice. It was just her mother's way. Elisabeth couldn't remember her mother ever spanking her, although she had received some harsh scoldings at times.

"Ma, he was arguing with a man just now, trying to buy his mules too cheap," Elisabeth said. It was obvious who the *he* was. "And a stranger was out there." Elisabeth automatically glanced over her shoulder, although she knew the stranger was gone. "He was a missionary. Ma, what is a missionary?"

"You remember the Tillotsons who stayed a few days with us. They were missionaries."

"I know. I remember them. But what I mean is, exactly what do they do?"

"Well," Mary paused from her work, staring thoughtfully into space for a moment. "They're usually sent by their home church to spread the word of God, to deliver Bibles, help those in need. That sort of thing."

Elisabeth thought about that as she grabbed an apron and whisked it over her head. The man had kind eyes, she remembered; he would be good at his work, she was sure. "Missionaries go to different parts of the country?" she asked.

"I think they have certain territories they're responsible for." She glanced back at her daughter. "You must have been quite taken with the man."

Elisabeth nodded slowly. "I was. He seemed like a gentleman," she said, tying the apron strings as her mind drifted to the normal flow of people at the post. "Ma, I'm tired of all these drifters," she said impulsively. "They're rude, they spit tobacco juice on the walk, and they stare and use bad grammar."

"That's why I'm paying that uppity Eastern lady to teach you. Lucky for us, her husband got down on his luck and they ended up here instead of Pueblo. She's been a real blessing."

Elisabeth nodded, thinking that Alice Stacker had influenced her life more than anyone she knew. Mrs. Stacker was soft-spoken, cultured, and once a beauty, though she was quickly aging here in the west.

"I want a better life for you," Mary said, her hand resting on the dough as her eyes stared dreamily into space.

"Maybe I'll meet a rich man," Elisabeth teased, feeling the oppression of the morning pass as she and her mother engaged in one of their dreaming sessions. "That man will fall in love with me and then we'll—"

"*Indians!*"

The hoarse shouts of warning reverberated over the peaceful post, bringing Mary and Elisabeth to the door.

A dozen Indians were galloping into the courtyard, scattering snow, dogs, and children in a wave of panic. They wore fringed buckskin and beaded headbands. One man, obviously the leader, wore a headdress of white feathers.

"They threatened to attack if they can't trade!" the guard at the gate was yelling.

The leader edged his white horse ahead of his braves as his eyes, black as midnight, scanned every building. There was something about him that commanded attention. He held his head high and proud, and his face bore a stony expression. It was an arresting face—lean, taut skin over rigid bones, a prominent nose, and piercing black eyes. He drew up before the hitching rail of the general store as his braves fanned out around him.

Jed Greenwood threw open the door and scrambled onto the boardwalk, gaping at the startling sight before him. The cold black eyes that swept Greenwood flashed contempt as Lone Eagle shifted on his horse and coolly surveyed the gawking crowd. A few men took a step closer, curiously inspecting the formidable Indian chief as he motioned to a young brave.

The brave dropped down from his horse and removed an armload of buffalo hides. Jed's jaw sagged at the sight of the hides, so hard to come by now. Another brave followed with beadwork, water-jug baskets, and wooden flutes.

"You want to trade, Chief?" Jed yelled, a wicked gleam rising in his narrow-set eyes.

Lone Eagle sat rigid on his white horse, whose muscles rippled beneath the firm hand of restraint. "The young squaw." Lone Eagle's deep voice boomed over the courtyard, quiet as death. "We trade for the young squaw."

"*Squaw?*" Jed croaked. "We got no squaw here!" His greedy eyes returned to the buffalo hides and the handmade pieces that would tantalize the miners into parting with their gold dust and coins. But this crazy Indian wanted a squaw!

"What about some white lightning from Taos, Chief?" Jed asked with a sly grin.

Lone Eagle glared at him. "Trapper John tell us papoose left at your wagon. Papoose belong to Morning Dove."

Jed sucked in his breath as his eyes slid to the kitchen where Mary and Elisabeth watched from the open door. Elisabeth! They wanted Elisabeth.

Jed clawed at the tight collar of his flannel shirt as he forced a hollow laugh from his tight throat.

"Chief, you got me confused with someone else. Why, I ain't been in no wagon train. I been at this post for eighteen years."

The muscles in Lone Eagle's face clenched as he ground his teeth together, and a murderous warning leapt into his black eyes.

"Morning Dove leave a papoose eighteen winters ago," he countered. "Morning Dove dying. She want squaw."

Shocked whispers flew over the crowd. Heads turned, eyes shot to the kitchen door, which suddenly closed. The old-timers had heard how the Greenwood's daughter had been left at their wagon, wrapped in an Indian blanket.

"You take," Lone Eagle said, motioning toward their offering placed on the steps of the store. "When the sun rise again, we come for squaw. No squaw. . ." he touched the pouch of arrows strapped to his side, "we fight."

He swung the big horse around and motioned to his braves. The hard-packed snow flew into the air, settling again into wet clumps as the horses thundered through the gate. As soon as the gate slammed shut, shouts of panic erupted across the post. Men cursed, women cried out in fear, and Tommy tore across the courtyard for the kitchen, yelling for

Elisabeth as he ran.

The sound of wood striking wood captured the attention of the shuffling crowd as the kitchen door was flung wide and banged against the wall. Mary marched out into the courtyard, her long skirts billowing in the wind, her plump hands still floured and thrust in determined fists on her large hips.

"Nobody's proved Elisabeth belongs to this Indian woman!" she yelled, her pale blue eyes moving over each face in the crowd. "Why, she's lighter skinned than half of you! They just want her, that's all. They've seen her and they want her."

"Mary, why start a war over it?" someone yelled. "Couldn't Elisabeth just visit the old squaw? Be nice to her, then come on back to the post?"

"No!"

"Are you askin' us to fight 'em off, then?" A small, scowling man stepped forward. " 'Cause we got a war on our hands come sunrise if we don't figger somethin' out."

"I'll not turn my daughter over to them!" Mary shouted, her voice and her eyes daring anyone to challenge her. "And that's final!" She whirled and lumbered back inside, her large body stiff with pride. But her spine felt the cold breath of terror, a terror that surpassed all other terrors of her life.

Her steps quickened until she was almost running by the time she reached the kitchen. Her hands trembled on the door latch, trembled even more as she slammed it and shot the bolt. She turned slowly, dreading to face Elisabeth, who was now pacing the floor, wringing her hands.

"Here now," Mary laid a protective arm around her shoulder, "don't look so scared, honey. Nobody's taking you away."

"Is it true?" Elisabeth demanded. "Am I the daughter of Morning Dove?"

"Course not!" Mary began to pace the floor with her. "They just watched you from the cliffs and want you—like all red-blooded males!" She yanked a stray hair back into her bun. "Why, the Cheyennes and Arapahoes are attacking wagon trains and taking the women home as squaws. The Utes are getting ideas now. But they'll not get you, baby."

Pulling her daughter close to her, Mary could feel the erratic pounding of her own heart. Fear clutched at her chest, choking the air from her lungs. She drew a slow, measured breath and forced a smile to her stiff lips. "I love you as my own. They'll not get you!"

"Ma, I don't want anyone killed because of me," Elisabeth protested, anxiously rubbing her forehead, trying to think. "Maybe I should go."

"No! You're not that squaw's daughter. And they'll keep you once they get you into their camp. I've heard the miners and trappers talking. The

Indians want white women."

She paused to catch her breath. "You were kidnapped from another wagon train," she said forcefully, her tone more rational. "We all knew that."

A fist pounded the door. "Open up, Mary," Jed yelled. "We gotta do something."

As she unbolted the door and he burst into the kitchen, a torrent of words spilled from his mouth. "Them savages may not wait until sunrise. They may get a hankerin' to come back tonight."

Jed rarely wore a hat, and his thinning gray hair now stood on end. He tugged at his nose, marbled with broken blood vessels. "Her features ain't Indian, and her skin ain't real dark, but her hair and eyes. . ." He was muttering his thoughts aloud, distressing Mary even more.

Her hands clutched and unclutched the folds of her apron. "It's the craziest thing I ever heard, Jed. Elisabeth, an Indian."

"Well, she was wrapped in an Indian blanket, remember? You always figgered she was stolen, but . . ." his voice trailed off as he stared at Elisabeth's features, then the shape of her long slim body, examining her as though she were a stranger. "How did that Indian know a baby was put at our wagon if the ma didn't tell him?" he asked Mary.

"They just want her and they'll lie to get her," Mary snapped, beads of perspiration breaking over her upper lip. "All that matters is, she's *our* daughter now. So help me, they ain't getting her."

Jed's eyes narrowed on his wife while his mind pondered the value of those buffalo skins, buffalo so hard to come by now! And the trinkets and beads—why, he could make a hefty profit in no time.

His eyes shot back to Elisabeth. If she belonged to the Indians by blood, why start a war over it? He scowled and shook his head. Then turning to open the door, he stormed out.

"He'll trade me," Elisabeth's voice was a mere whisper as she stared at the space where Jed had stood.

"He'll do no such thing!" Mary cried. "I'm going to find Trapper John and get to the bottom of this."

≈

Trapper John was a slight yet hardy man in his sixties. A grizzled gray beard and sideburns covered most of his thin weathered face. Straggly white hair fell from beneath his coonskin cap, brushing the collar of his rabbit-skin jacket. He had survived blizzards, famine on a wagon train, and had even been trapped in a cave to escape a hungry mountain lion—and it all showed in his leathery face.

But nothing equaled the threat in Mary's face as she poked a loaded musket into his chest, backing him against the slab wood of the horse corral.

"Tell me what you told them, and for once you'd

better get your story straight!"

Constant exposure to bitter wind and summer sun had weathered and darkened John's skin to the bronze hue of the Cheyenne. All color drained from his face, however, as the tip of the barrel slammed against his breastbone.

"I been tradin' with Lone Eagle for years, Mary," he sputtered. "His camp's half a day south of here. He's been pestering me lately about a young squaw that one of his braves seen here at the post. I just figgered the brave was hankering after her, that's all. I thought. . ." His teeth ground into his bottom lip as he struggled to reason out the words before he spoke them.

"You thought what?" Mary challenged.

Trapper John took a deep breath that made a choked hiss in the night silence, tense with the shocking news. Everyone seemed to be waiting with bated breath to see what the Greenwoods would do.

"I thought if he knew she was forsook by her parents like there was something wrong with her. . . Mary, you know how superstitious them Indians are. I figured if he thought somethin' was wrong with her, he'd stop asking."

"So did he?" Each word was like a stone hurled in his face.

"No." A heavy sigh wrenched John's thin frame. "Then Lone Eagle told me his sister was dying.

That she thought all her pain was coming from the Great Spirit for leaving that baby at the palefaces' wagon." The words fell over his tongue, unchecked. "The squaw never could have babies after that, he told me. He said. . ."

"He said what?" Mary poked the gun farther into his chest. Her face was ashen, her heart hammered.

"He said the squaw Morning Dove wanted him to bring that baby back. She knew about you folks. She must have kept an eye on your wagon. She knew you were here."

Mary slumped, defeat registering in her eyes as she stared blindly into space.

Seeing her grip on the gun lighten and the look on her face, as though someone had dealt her a blow, John grabbed a breath and made another attempt to rectify the situation.

"Lone Eagle said the squaw wants to see the girl before she dies. Maybe that's all there is to it, Mary," he finished lamely.

She sank back against the wall of the corral as a hard pain tore through the center of her chest. She lowered the musket.

"Mary, you better get ahold of yourself," John said, suddenly concerned. "You look like your heart's about to take out on you."

"Not yet," she hissed. She had to think what to do. She had to save Elisabeth. But how? She lifted a hand to her heart, pressing against the persistent ache. The damage was done, and of course she had no intention of shooting John, although she felt tempted. But he would pay for his mistake later, she would see to that.

"I'm sorry, Mary," he muttered softly. "If only I could have done something—"

"You can do something now," she snapped. "You can take her to Denver tonight."

"Tonight?" John choked, his eyes shooting to the mass of dark clouds rolling in on a northern wind.

"You can take the best horses, and I'll pack food and coffee."

"Denver," he repeated limply. "That's all night and into tomorrow."

"You'll do it, John, and don't tell me you won't. You got that poor girl into this mess and you're gonna get her out." She raised the musket again.

John gulped and nodded. "All right, Mary. Get her ready. We'll head out within the hour."

Mary heaved a sigh of relief, then glanced worriedly at the clouds in the night sky. "The Tillotson family lives on this side of Denver. They're missionaries. They spent some time here, and I nursed his wife through a bad stomach ailment. They said if I ever needed anything. . ."

"Mary, what'll happen if Elisabeth ain't here when the Indians come back?" John didn't want to get killed, but he didn't want to be responsible for an Indian uprising at the post either.

Mary shook her head. "I don't know, and right now I don't care. I have to think of Elisabeth."

"Does Jed know you're planning to sneak her out?"

Mary glared at him, her fingers closing over the trigger of the musket.

He sighed. "I'll take her anyway."

three

Elisabeth huddled into her fur coat, her teeth chattering, her mind dazed with shock. In the darkness outside the corral, Trapper John led out a gentle mare, then turned back to a frisky roan, raising the stirrups to accommodate his short legs.

"Now, don't waste any time," Mary whispered through the darkness, tucking a bundle of food in John's saddlebags.

"I'll send you a message from town," John said, pulling up into the saddle and lowering his cap against the wind.

"You'll be okay, honey," Mary said, her eyes hungrily searching Elisabeth's face as though memorizing each feature.

"Yes, I know. Don't worry about me," Elisabeth answered, trying to be brave.

"Elisabeth, you keep a tight rein on that mare," John warned from behind her. "We'll just mosey quiet-like out the gate and across them foothills. That's the best way to slip outta this valley."

Mary's plump hand shot up to grip Elisabeth's arm. "The Tillotsons are good people. They'll take care of you, and I'll come as soon as I can."

Elisabeth's teeth were chattering, more from nerves than cold, as she nodded in agreement, glancing one last time at the log buildings huddled in a dark mass against the falling snow.

"Take care of yourself, Ma," Elisabeth said, her eyes returning to Mary, always so strong, yet reduced to heaving sobs now. The sight brought tears to Elisabeth's eyes, but she sank her teeth into her lower lip, refusing to break down. She gripped the reins and kneed her mare into line behind Sam.

The guard opened the gate, a sad smile on his face as he quietly waved them through.

❧

Elisabeth shivered even in her coat, her eyes stinging from the tears she fought to control. Her bottom lip ached from the hard thrust of her teeth as she centered her thoughts on getting to Denver. Her eyes were focused determinedly on Trapper John, whose cap was drawn low over his head. Just beneath the bottom edge of the hat, his earlobes glistened fire-red from the cold.

The mare plodded along, its slow, easy rhythm a soothing distraction to her turbulent thoughts. For the past hours, her mind had been frozen in shock. She was relieved that her mother had taken charge, making all the decisions for her. Now, as she rode along in the darkened night, the cold air had a sobering effect, mobilizing her thoughts again.

What if Lone Eagle spoke the truth? How could she know what to believe? Her mother seemed certain that the Indians had kidnapped her from another wagon train, but was that what had *really* happened?

≥

They had ridden in silence for almost an hour when Elisabeth sensed a change in the quiet night. She studied John up ahead of her, huddled against the cold. He seemed unaware of any change, yet her skin prickled. What was wrong, what was different?

The silence was no longer complete. That was it! She pushed her hood back and strained to hear. Then the change she had tried to identify became apparent even to John, who wheeled his horse around. The leather of his saddle creaked as he shifted his weight to survey the darkness that enclosed them, a darkness feathered by gently falling snow.

Elisabeth pulled her mare to a halt, following Sam's searching gaze into the black night and seeing nothing. But there was a sound drifting through the darkness, a thudding that grew stronger—hoofbeats, muffled by snow.

"Someone's after us," John called at the moment the realization struck her. "And we ain't hanging around to find out who! Kick that mare and ride like the wind!" he yelled. "We gotta reach them rocks up there so we can hide."

Wordlessly, she obeyed, slamming her booted heels into the mare's sides. The horse lunged forward, and the snow spun a white web around her as the mare tore across the frozen earth. Elisabeth's pulse drummed in her ears as she struggled to hang on, while the cold wind stung her face and blurred her vision.

The night was suddenly rent with shouts, words that were foreign to her. Then suddenly a body had landed on top of John, knocking him from his horse and into the snow.

"John!" she screamed, jerking the reins. At her panicked tugging, the mare reared, then plunged again, throwing Elisabeth headlong into the snow.

She was half-buried in a mound that froze her face and matted her lashes. She struggled to get up, impatiently brushing the wetness from her face.

Hoofbeats and wild shouts filled her ears as she shook loose the clumps that clung to her clothes. A rough hand yanked her to her feet, snapping her head back, and suddenly she was staring into the dark face of an Indian brave.

"John!" she glanced back over her shoulder, trying to see what had happened to him as more faces crowded in. Dark eyes peered at her as though she were a creature from another world.

She glanced across the snow, looking for Trapper John. They had not harmed him, she was relieved to see that. Two braves were merely restraining him as a hand gripped her and strong arms returned her to her horse. There was no point in asking where she was going, for she already knew.

Lone Eagle had won after all.

four

Moonlight streamed over the mountains, turning the peaks to a gleaming silver as the Indians led Elisabeth's mare into a wide meadow enclosed by dark pine forests and jagged boulders. This was the land of the bubbling springs that she'd heard about, where Utes left trinkets for the Great Spirit. She remembered a trapper who had once stolen one of those trinkets and had come to the post with it. Jed had traded some flour and sugar for it, put it in a jar, and told everyone it was a valuable good-luck charm from a medicine man. A Kansas mule-skinner turned gold seeker had paid a fortune for it.

Half-frozen and numb with shock, Elisabeth stared through bleary eyes at the small, silent village where a campfire threw flickering shadows on the buckskin lodges clustered in a wide circle.

The lead Indian broke from the group and loped into camp, shouting hoarsely as he tumbled from his pinto and raced to a lodge in the center of the village.

Flaps were thrown back, faces peered into the

darkness, before torches were lit to flare in Elisabeth's terrified face.

Lone Eagle appeared, wearing a furry robe and a long, elk-tooth necklace. His black hair hung in thick braids bound by rawhide, which swung about his shoulders as he broke through the gathering crowd and approached her. His dark eyes held a look of triumph.

"Come!" he commanded.

The deep voice rumbled over her, sending chills down her spine. She dismounted, pulling her coat tightly around her. Every bone in her body ached and throbbed from the long, punishing ride and the freezing cold. Still, she held herself erect, not wanting the staring kidnappers to sense her fear. She followed Lone Eagle to a tall lodge that held colorful drawings of elk and deer. A large painting in the center featured a huge eagle and a young warrior.

Nearby, a smaller lodge held only one painting, that of a sad Indian maiden staring up at a dove on a tree limb. *Morning Dove,* she thought. Lone Eagle threw the flap back and motioned her inside.

Elisabeth hesitated, growing apprehensive. Then, feeling Lone Eagle's black eyes urging her on, she forced herself to enter the lodge. A flickering candle offset the darkness within, as she blinked and glanced around her. A young girl sat beside a small, thin body that lay still as death on a bed of animal skins.

"Morning Dove." Lone Eagle pointed, stepping toward the sick woman.

Elisabeth's feet were like stones as she edged toward the small woman whose gaunt brown face was as shriveled as the prunes they sold at the trading post. Her gray hair was swept back from her face in a single braid, and curiously, Elisabeth took a step closer, carefully studying the blunt nose, pale lips, and sunken cheeks. *This person could not possibly be my mother,* she thought, sighing with relief.

The woman appeared to be sleeping, but, as though sensing her presence, the sunken eyes began to open.

The big bronze chief leaned down and touched his sister's shoulder. He spoke in a low voice, words Elisabeth did not understand. Then suddenly the woman struggled to sit up; dark, pain-filled eyes flew to Elisabeth.

Elisabeth froze as a gnarled hand flailed through the air and the woman began to babble incoherently. The words died away and the woman lay with her mouth open, gasping for breath, as Elisabeth stared.

"Little Dove. Your name Little Dove," Lone Eagle's deep voice broke through Elisabeth's thoughts. "She say your spirit sings even when you suffer. Like the little dove."

Elisabeth's mouth dropped open as her eyes drifted back to the sick woman who was staring at her with a wide, toothless smile.

"But there's been a mistake," she burst out. "I'm not Little Dove. I'm Elisabeth Greenwood. And I'm not her daughter."

Lone Eagle's black eyes were as sharp as eagle eyes, and he glared threateningly at her. "Tell her you forgive."

Elisabeth gulped and looked from his stern face to the suffering woman. "I forgive you," she said, staring into Morning Dove's pain-filled eyes.

Lone Eagle translated her reply, and the woman listened carefully as tears filled her eyes and rolled unevenly down her creased cheeks.

Watching her, Elisabeth felt a sudden surge of pity for this woman, Morning Dove. Even if she wasn't her mother, Elisabeth decided it would do no harm to be kind. She was obviously dying. Elisabeth studied the brown hand, dangling in midair. Shyly, she reached out and grasped the cold fingers. New strength seemed to flow into the woman's feeble body, and Morning Dove began to speak again.

Elisabeth frowned, carefully studying the sunken eyes, the nut-brown skin. No, this woman couldn't

possibly be her mother and yet—how did she know
that Elisabeth had been left beside a wagon?

The trauma of what was happening seemed to
center itself in one blinding pain behind her forehead. Elisabeth could no longer think straight; how
could she know what to believe?

Morning Dove's strange murmurings had ceased,
and the grasp on Elisabeth's hand weakened. An
expression of peace settled over Morning Dove's
features as she closed her eyes and slept again.

Lone Eagle nodded approval at Elisabeth, then
turned and swept out of the lodge.

Elisabeth's eyes cautiously followed. As the flap
closed behind him, she gently removed her hand
from Morning Dove's grasp.

The flap opened again, and the girl who had been
keeping vigil returned with a clay pot of steaming
broth. Elisabeth's eyes dropped to the thin liquid,
and her mouth began to water as her empty stomach
reacted to the flavorful aroma. She was motioned to
a corner of the lodge where a smooth rock served as
a table. She sank down on a buffalo skin, her weary
glance moving from the broth to the dark-skinned
girl, who gave her a shy smile before she darted out
again.

Elisabeth filled her stomach, trying not to think.
But one worry after another raced through her mind.
What happened to Trapper John? Did he return

he lit out in another direction, afraid to admit his mission had failed? What was going to happen to her?

She glanced around the small lodge, walled with buffalo hides sewn together between long, rigid poles that narrowed into a chimney at the top. The lining of the skins helped insulate the lodge against the harsh weather, but Elisabeth continued to shiver. As her eyes moved curiously about, she could see doeskin dresses, moccasins beaded in flower designs, and baskets shaped like jugs attached to the poles. Along the floor, there were more baskets of various sizes and shapes, and a clay bowl and crude wooden spoon.

Elisabeth sighed and returned to her broth. As she was finishing, the flap parted and the Indian girl returned, carrying a buckskin dress, a pair of moccasins, and several animal skins, which she indicated was to be Elisabeth's bed.

Bone-weary, Elisabeth sank onto the skins, too numb in mind and body to care what would happen next. The warm broth had filled her hungry stomach, and with only the snores of the sick woman to distract her, she pulled the extra skins over her and quickly fell asleep.

ه

Elisabeth huddled before the morning fire, staring glumly at the interior of Morning Dove's lodge. Ab-

glumly at the interior of Morning Dove's lodge. Absently, she counted thirteen slim poles that held the dried buffalo hides together. Her eyes roamed to the opening covered with a flap of skin held by two rigid poles. If only she could walk through that opening and leave this village behind. But an Indian brave stood guard outside, making her their prisoner.

She sighed and turned to stare into the fire. She was trapped within this lodge, this village. And to complicate matters, one of the braves had become a suitor of sorts. Still, she had refused to wear the clothes of an Indian maiden, chosen to eat and sleep in her one rumpled dresses until this morning when Lone Eagle had demanded she wear the dress and moccasins they had given her.

Her eyes ran down the soft buckskin dress now, ending on her moccasined feet. She was beginning to feel like one of them, and she had noticed that her hair was as dark as many of the other maidens. Was it true that her father had been white, had actually raped Morning Dove, who had then left Elisabeth with the white people?

She had been told this over the past week, and at times she half believed it. But another part of her mind argued that this could not possibly be true.

She sat brooding, staring listlessly into the fire. Homesick tears welled in her eyes. Five days had passed, and the tense waiting had drained her energy. The Utes interpreted her silence as submission to this strange life, but they were wrong.

Her pent-up tears overflowed and streamed down her cheeks when she thought of the post and her adoptive parents. Surely by now they had heard from Trapper John that she had not reached Denver—if John were alive to tell them! Surely Ma knew they had not reached the Tillotsons for there had been no telegraph back to assure her. Elisabeth expected little from Jed Greenwood, but her ma. . .

She wandered over to lift the flap, trying to push those thoughts from her troubled mind as she studied the inhabitants of Lone Eagle's small village. On this cold morning, the men wore animal skin robes over their breechcloths and moccasins. The women wore loose dresses fashioned from animal skins. Some of the dresses held painted decorations; a few were embroidered with beads. The women talked in low voices, smiling at one another, apparently happy in their work.

Near the fire, some of the women were skinning a large buck brought in from the morning hunt. Two squaws had cradleboards strapped to their backs. The dark-eyed babies appeared content, obviously accustomed to this kind of activity. The children roamed freely. A few were clustered together in some sort of game with a stick and a rock. Their dark braids bounced against their rabbit-skin coats as they raced merrily about.

Strange, Elisabeth thought, *how the children here seem happier than those at the post.* None cried or begged at their mother's side. Suddenly, one of the children let out an excited shriek and jabbed a small finger in the direction of the trail leading into camp. The other children joined in the excitement, laughing and yelling as they raced toward the road.

Elisabeth's brow knitted in a curious frown, and she ventured outside to investigate. Everyone's attention was centered on a man riding a black stallion into the village.

Recognition flashed in Elisabeth's eyes. It was him! The missionary who had come to the post. Had her parents sent him to speak with Lone Eagle? For the first time since her capture, her hopes soared.

The children crowded about him as he swung down from his horse and reached into his saddlebags. Hands shot out, eagerly awaiting the contents. Obviously, this man was no stranger here; certainly he must have been generous in the past. The children shrieked with delight as their small hands were filled with peppermint sticks and assorted trinkets.

She studied the man more closely. A friendly smile touched his lips as he spoke to the children. Elisabeth stepped outside, staring curiously at this man who had stood up to her father, as few men did, yet who could be generous and caring to the Indian children.

"How!"

The deep voice of Lone Eagle rumbled as he swept past her. For the first time, there was a pleasant expression on his face as he looked from the man to the children who were jumping up and down with glee.

"How!" The stranger called back, lifting his hand. As the missionary returned Lone Eagle's greeting, he did not seem intimidated by the Indian Chief. Still, he spoke with respect, half in English, half in the Ute language, as Lone Eagle approached his side.

As the sunlight filtered over the man who had so fascinated her, Elisabeth took in every detail of his appearance. His rugged features and buckskin clothes made him the epitome of the western man, yet the brown eyes held a look of humility as he spoke words of kindness to the children who flocked around him. As she stood staring, he glanced in her direction, and she saw a look of surprise flash over his face. But then Lone Eagle spoke, reclaiming his attention.

Elisabeth's brave smile began to waver. She had expected him to acknowledge her in some way if, indeed, he had been sent to take her home. But then she recalled his disagreement with her father. What, she wondered, had Jed offered him to come here for her? Maybe it was part of his plan, to appear casual, conceal his real intention.

When he turned to walk with Lone Eagle to the center lodge, Elisabeth motioned to Deer Woman.

"Who is he?" she asked, pointing to the tall handsome man.

"Friend. . ." The old woman spoke the word slowly, reverently, as she touched a thin silver bracelet on her wrist.

Elisabeth's eyes jumped from the bracelet back to Lone Eagle's lodge, into which the men had disappeared. Just then a wail of pain pierced the air, and Elisabeth turned back into Morning Dove's lodge. The woman's agonizing battle for life appeared to be coming to an end. Her dark eyes rolled back in her head, and the mouth that had issued moans of agony now sagged as Morning Dove sank into death.

Elisabeth stared down at her, dumbfounded at the reality of death, even a death that had been obviously imminent. She heard someone speaking rapidly, and she turned to see Deer Woman's aging eyes widening in stunned comprehension as she stared at Morning Dove's lifeless body. Then she dashed out, shrieking the news.

Gently, Elisabeth pulled the buffalo robe over Morning Dove's still face, and as she did, she was surprised to feel sadness welling up inside of her. She thought of what Lone Eagle had said, that Morning Dove was her mother. She shook her head slowly, dismissing that unlikely possibility. There was not the slightest resemblance. It had all been a mistake, as her mother had insisted.

Lone Eagle burst into the lodge, his dark face filled with sorrow at the sight of his sister's covered body. Elisabeth could see the buckskin trousers of the stranger at the edge of the flap, as he politely waited outside. She glanced back at Lone Eagle, who was momentarily caught up in grief.

Seizing the opportunity, she slipped from the lodge and motioned the stranger out of earshot of Lone Eagle.

"I'm Elisabeth Greenwood from Greenwood's Trading Post," she spoke breathlessly, eagerly awaiting his reaction.

"I'm Adam Pearson. The people here call me Walks Tall." He smiled. Removing his skin cap, he looked into her face. Elisabeth's eyes ran over his slim smooth features—thick brows over deep-set brown eyes, straight nose and sculpted lips, and a firm jawline. His skin was deeply tanned, and she noticed a slight cleft in his chin. Her eyes moved down the muscled neck, swept broad shoulders, narrow torso and long legs, ending in dark leather boots. She shook her head slightly, trying to pull her thoughts back to her reason for speaking to him.

"Did my parents send you?" she whispered.

"*Send* me?" he tilted his head, obviously unclear as to what she was talking about.

Elisabeth swallowed, fighting the sick disappointment overtaking her. "I've been kidnapped," she explained desperately. "I'm Jed Greenwood's daughter from the post. You were there. I saw you!"

"Kidnapped?" he repeated, as though nothing else she had said registered in his mind. "I can't believe Lone Eagle would allow—"

"There's been a terrible mistake," Elisabeth interrupted, glancing impatiently toward the lodge. "I haven't time to explain but you must believe me." Her hand shot out, grasping desperately at his fringed sleeve. "You must help me. *Please.*"

His eyes widened, taking in every inch of her, from her tangled hair down the buckskin dress to her dusty moccasins, as Lone Eagle emerged from the lodge.

"She has gone to the Great Spirit," he said, heaving a sigh.

"Lone Eagle, may I say a prayer for her?" Adam

asked gently.

Elisabeth stared at him. Why did he want to say a prayer for her? Did missionaries act as ministers also?

"Would you allow me to do that?" Adam persisted.

Lone Eagle nodded and Adam stepped inside the lodge. As he did, Lone Eagle turned his attention to Elisabeth.

While their dark eyes locked, she heard the gentle tones being spoken inside the lodge.

"I want to go home," she spoke in a small yet firm voice. "I have cared for her as you asked; I have told her I forgive her. Now my people will be worried."

At that moment, Adam had stepped outside the lodge again and was looking curiously at Elisabeth and then Lone Eagle.

"I think this man will be willing to see me back to the post. Please let me go!" she cried, her eyes filling with tears.

Lone Eagle merely grunted and turned to motion Adam toward his lodge.

Adam stared at her for a moment, obviously puzzled by all he had encountered. When he turned and strode after Lone Eagle, Elisabeth suddenly realized she hadn't even asked him to take her home. Surely she could persuade him to do that;

her parents would pay him well, she was sure of that.

But what if he was going in another direction? What if he refused?

five

Elisabeth stared after them as they disappeared into Lone Eagle's lodge. Gripping her hands tightly against her waist, she suddenly became aware of the dirt on her skin. She looked down at her broken grimy nails. No wonder Adam Pearson was reluctant to help her. She yanked a strand of hair from her shoulder, examining its dull, lifeless color. Why, she looked like a vagabond, she looked. . .like a squaw, only these squaws were cleaner than she was.

Footsteps whispered behind her, and she whirled to see Deer Woman returning to Morning Dove's lodge. Sighing, Elisabeth stepped inside, determined to find a way to say good-bye and leave with Adam. Deer Woman was gathering up Morning Dove's clay bowl, her beaded moccasins, and doeskin dress.

"What are you doing?" Elisabeth asked curiously.

Deer Woman motioned to the lifeless body, then held the articles up and indicated through hand motions that these would be buried in the crevice of the red rocks with Morning Dove.

Elisabeth nodded. Unlike their Cheyenne neighbors who buried their dead high above the ground, the Utes buried their people in rock crevices, and they particularly favored the high red rocks.

A low, mournful wail broke over the camp. Other voices joined in, and soon the sound of dozens of stamping feet filled her ears. A chant swept over the village; this was the mourning dance she had heard about at the post.

The tent flap was thrown back and two braves entered.

Elisabeth quickly looked away, unable to watch as they hoisted the lifeless body and carried it from the lodge.

Watching them go, a strange emotion began to sweep over her. She had developed a feeling for this woman over the past days, one she had not yet identified. When she first came here, she had known that the woman's death might permit her to return to the post; now, there was an odd hollow feeling, an emptiness welling up inside. Why did she feel this way? Her mother had once told her that folks didn't always understand what went on in the heart. She had thought the words strange at the time, but now they made sense to her.

She frowned, following the men from the lodge. As she stood on the edge of the crowd, her eyes met those of the brave who had been boldly watching her all week. Her breath caught.

She had to do something; she had to act now before the brave persuaded Lone Eagle to keep her here.

Her decision propelled her feet into action, and she flew up the path to Lone Eagle's lodge and burst in, surprising Lone Eagle and Adam as they sat quietly smoking the pipe.

She clenched her fists at her sides, summoning all her courage. "Let me go," she said, her voice shaky yet determined. "Please let me go. She's dead now. There's nothing more I can do here."

Lone Eagle's face was a bronze mask.

Adam Pearson laid down the pipe and rose to his feet. "Perhaps I can settle the problem," he said pleasantly. "The God I worship does not believe in holding people against their will. If you will let her return to the people who care for her, I am willing to make a trade." He reached into his pocket. "I panned many streams for this." He withdrew a gold nugget, offering it to Lone Eagle.

Lone Eagle's dark eyes glowed as he turned the nugget over in his palm, studying its soft gleam in the glow of the fire.

For a moment, Elisabeth's eyes were frozen in shock as she, too, stared at the nugget. How humiliating to be traded for a. . .a piece of rock!

"You don't have to do that," she said sharply, her

eyes relaying her offense.

Adam did not respond, he merely looked back at Lone Eagle.

"Do we trade?" he asked.

Lone Eagle's eyes swept Elisabeth. "You want to go back to them?" he asked sharply.

"Yes, I do. They raised me. They're my family now."

With a sigh he began to nod. "Then we trade."

six

The sun was not yet midway across the sky when Elisabeth climbed on her horse again and rode off with Adam. She had changed back into the rumpled clothes she had worn for days, but she had managed to bathe and redo her hair.

Neither she nor Adam spoke as their horses plodded away from the camp. She dared not look back, though many eyes followed them.

"Where do you come from?" she asked, shifting nervously in the saddle. She hoped to make conversation and put the unpleasant situation behind them as soon as possible.

"I was raised in the south." He looked across at her. "But I've been in Colorado for three years. I ride the circuit, visiting people throughout the territory. I also pan a little and trap a little to make ends meet."

"My father will repay you for the nugget," she pushed her chin forward stubbornly, still embarrassed by the incident.

His dark eyes returned to her, and she could see that he was puzzled by what she had said.

"What really happened?" he asked, turning back to straighten the reins in his hands as their horses walked at a leisurely pace through the deep snow.

"You mean why was I kidnapped by the Indians?" She sighed. "I was hoping you had been sent by my father."

She glanced at him and saw that his head was tilted; the dark eyes were sweeping over her curiously once again. She felt her skin flushing beneath his gaze, and she looked away.

Her mother's stern protectiveness had discouraged most of the single males who came to the post. Mary didn't consider any of them good enough for her daughter. There had been only two who may have proved acceptable suitors, but the trains had moved on, and there had been no time for a friendship to develop.

Now she felt painfully vulnerable and inexperienced.

"I wasn't sent," he answered her. "Sorry to disappoint you. I stop in on Lone Eagle's camp when I am in the territory. Part of my mission is to help the Indians."

She bit her lip, considering his words. What would he think if he knew they considered her to be Ute? As though reading her thoughts, he spoke again, shocking her with his words.

"My mother was a Cherokee in North Carolina;

my father was a pioneer. They married and I was their only child. We lived in the wilderness until my mother died. Then he moved into town so I could attend school," he spoke matter-of-factly, as if this bit of information was old news. "My father's brother was a missionary to Colorado. I was fascinated by his stories when he came back to visit. I began to do some missionary work among the Cherokees. Then later I came here."

She turned to stare at him, amazed by what he had told her. Then, before thinking, she spoke her observation.

"You seem proud to be—" She bit her lip, hating herself for so blatantly revealing her emotions.

"To be part Cherokee? Yes, I'm proud of my heritage," he said, looking across at her. Then slowly a dark shadow seemed to pass over his face. "One of the most tragic things I can think of is being ashamed of the life God has given you."

"My life hasn't been that good," she said, fighting back the sudden rush of tears. The dense woods bordering the road blurred before her, as she fought to control her emotions. "I never knew who my real parents were. I was left at a wagon train, wrapped in an Indian blanket. . . ."

"How did your parents explain that?" he asked.

Her stomach fluttered. It felt as though every nerve in her body were in a warfare in her stomach.

She swallowed and tried to keep her voice calm as she spoke. "My mother said I was kidnapped from one wagon train and delivered to another by the Indians."

He was thoughtful for a moment, staring at the snow-packed trail as they rode along. "I've never heard of that happening," he said quietly. "Usually if the Indians take a baby, they keep it. Many of the women lose their babies to sickness and are lonely for children."

"Well, that isn't what happened to me," she answered quickly. "Listen, I'm worried about the man who was taking me to Denver. Everyone called him Trapper John. Do you know him?"

"No, I don't believe I do."

"I wonder what happened to him." Her eyes were worried. "Either he died there in the snow or he lit out to Denver, afraid to tell Ma what really happened."

"And what did?"

Slowly, she began the story, telling him everything. As she did, she recalled how the people at the post had reacted when Lone Eagle announced she was the daughter of Morning Dove. Despite her mother's stern rebuttal, she had felt a change in the attitude of those around her. She sensed their doubt and suspicion, even among those she considered her friends. For as long as she could remember, people at the post scorned half-breeds. But this man didn't seem at all worried about that. He said he was proud of his heritage. She finished her story, leading up to this morning when he arrived. "So you see why I was desperate."

He looked at her. "Did they treat you well at the camp?"

She shrugged. "I can't complain." She was ashamed to admit to him how well she had been treated. Everyone had been kind to her, bringing her food and fresh clothing if she had wanted a change, but she didn't. She had even started refusing food.

"They were only kind to me because they thought I was her daughter," she said.

"They've always treated me very well." He said nothing more, but it was apparent to Elisabeth that he had great respect for Lone Eagle and his people. Possibly more respect than for Jed, whom he had caught trying to cheat a man.

"How far is it to the post?" she asked, shading her eyes against the white glare of sun on snow.

"We're half a day. If you want to, we can move at a faster pace."

"I want to," she said, kneeing her mare. "I'm eager to get *home*," she said, adding new emphasis to the word.

❧

Elisabeth's heart was lodged in her throat when

finally her eyes scanned the valley and came to rest on the trading post. Her hand automatically gripped the reins tighter, slowing her mare.

"What's wrong?" Adam asked, noting the change in her expression. Elisabeth swallowed. "I don't know. I'm just nervous, I guess."

As they neared the post, she began to smooth her wrinkled dress. Then she removed a comb from her saddlebags and whisked her hair into a bun at the nape of her neck. Although Elisabeth would not admit it, she was trying *not* to look like the Utes.

"I feel anxious about returning," she confessed. "I don't understand why Ma didn't send someone to Lone Eagle's camp. I didn't expect Jed to do anything, but Ma. . ." her voice trailed away as her eyes focused on the approaching pine buildings. Smoke curled high in the sky on this sunny morning. *Perhaps the sunshine is a good omen,* she thought.

As their horses trotted through the gate, Elisabeth's face fell at the meager greeting offered by a small group of stunned faces.

Adam's eyes drifted over the men, reading something more than shock in their expressions. Pity? Embarrassment?

Elisabeth drew rein at the post kitchen and dropped down.

"Ma!" she called, throwing open the kitchen door. She stopped in her tracks as a Mexican woman, years younger than her mother, looked up from the stove.

"Where's Ma?" Elisabeth asked, glancing around.

The kitchen was different in a way she couldn't immediately define. The smells were spicier; pots and pans cluttered the countertops. This was a stark contrast to Mary's neat kitchen.

She turned questioning eyes to the woman, who stood twisting her plump hands in her apron.

"You are. . .Elisabeth?"

She nodded, puzzled.

The woman dropped her head. "Your mother. . .is not here."

Elisabeth whirled from the kitchen and hurried across the courtyard to the cabin, her eyes flicking from right to left. Where were the children? Where was Tommy? Where was her mother?

"Ma?" she called, bursting into the cabin, ready to hurl herself against the bosom of the woman who had given her so much love. After what she'd been through, she felt that she needed Mary more than ever in her life.

Clothing was scattered carelessly about the cabin. On the wooden floor, snow clumps had melted to puddles of water. Lifting her skirts to sidestep the water, Elisabeth peered into the bedroom. She found only an empty, unmade bed. Frustration mounted as she flung open the door to her room.

Her mother was not there. A strange comb and brush and a black-lacquered hand mirror cluttered the tiny dresser.

Shocked, Elisabeth walked over to peer into the closet. The heavy perfume of the Spanish woman clung to the unfamiliar dresses hanging there.

A gentle rap sounded at the front door, and she found Adam standing on the slab step, his eyes filled with concern.

"May I come in?" he asked.

She nodded blankly, glancing back at the disheveled room. "I don't know what's going on. Ma's not here. . . ."

The sound of quick steps crunched over the snow beyond the open door, echoing in the tense silence that hung between Elisabeth and Adam. Then Jed Greenwood poked his head in the door.

"Thought you were in Denver."

"No. Didn't Trapper John come back and tell you? We never made it. Lone Eagle's braves were waiting for us. They took me back to camp. I don't know what happened to Trapper John. Either he died, or he rode on to avoid trouble with you."

Jed looked shocked at her words; he obviously knew nothing of what had happened.

"Where's Ma?" Elisabeth asked, as her eyes traveled nervously over the cluttered cabin. Behind the forced smile, her words held the echo of fear, a fear too horrible to identify.

Jed rubbed his hands down the front of his faded flannel shirt, casting a curious glance at Adam.

"Gone to Denver?" she asked. "Did she go to the Tillotsons looking for me? She said she would."

Jed coughed uncomfortably and loosened the collar of his shirt.

"Girl, I don't know how to say it, other than straight out." The silence in the room lengthened; only the steady drip of snow melting from the eaves outside could be heard for several seconds. Elisabeth's eyes darted to Adam as he took a step toward her.

"Your ma's heart give out the night you left," he finally blurted. "We buried her the next day."

"Buried her?" Elisabeth gasped, horrified. Buried her. . .?

Her hands flew to her mouth to stifle the sobs. Through a blur of tears, she saw Adam reach for her hand while Jed backed out the door.

"We never heard nothin'," Jed argued. "Figured you were safe in Denver. Thought it was best not to send for you, all things considered."

"What things?" Elisabeth gasped. "You should have known I'd want to be at Ma's funeral." She couldn't believe that the one person who had loved her was gone. She felt an arm slip around her shoulders, and she leaned against it, fearing her legs would buckle. Her ma *gone. Buried.*

Wiping the streaming tears, Elisabeth struggled for words. "Did she. . .suffer?"

Jed shook his head. "She just come in here," his eyes slid to the door of the room that had belonged to Mary, "laid down on the bed. . .and died."

Fresh tears stung Elisabeth's eyes and then as her gaze dropped to the floor she saw a tattered black lace petticoat. Her grief burst into rage. She snatched the petticoat from the floor, and hurled it against the wall. Then she spun on Jed. "And you moved that Mexican woman into Ma's house?"

"Elisabeth," Adam warned gently.

"Watch your mouth, girl," Jed snarled. "I had to have a cook."

"I can cook," she cried. "If only you'd sent for me—"

"I ain't gonna stir up war with them savages! Can't you get that through your head?" His eyes raked her in a slow contemptuous manner. "Besides, from what that Indian chief said, you may be the daughter of that squaw."

The room was spinning around her. She felt as though the earth had given way and she was being sucked down into the recesses of it. She would not let Jed Greenwood destroy her—she would not!

She forced herself to meet Jed's hard eyes. This was no longer her home. She knew that now, but she had to make an effort to stand her ground.

"I have spent the past week at Lone Eagle's camp," she answered, her voice taking on a calmer tone. "That squaw could not possibly be my mother." She waited for Jed's reaction, but his ex-pression remained unchanged. "Anyway, she died yester-day."

Jed said nothing; he merely glared at her.

Elisabeth studied his face with the wisdom of eighteen years spent cringing under his scowls. She stumbled across the living room and sank into a chair.

"I'd like to have something to remember Ma by," she said dully, staring at the dirty floorboards. "Then I'll be leaving."

If she had looked at Jed she would have caught the faint sigh of relief, followed by the twitch of satisfaction on his mouth. Adam, however, missed nothing.

"Her things is in a trunk in the other closet," Jed answered slowly. "Reckon you can have whatever you want." He paused to clear his throat. "Where are you going?"

Elisabeth lifted her tearstained face to him. Where indeed? She tried to think, but her mind was locked in disbelief.

"I could take you to Denver to the home of those folks you mentioned," Adam offered.

Jed's eyes flew back to Adam. He was obviously curious about this man who had brought her back, who had dared to speak up to him that day. But he certainly wasn't going to make a fuss; if the man was willing to get her off his hands, then so be it.

Elisabeth took a deep breath and looked at Adam. "Do you know the Tillotsons? They're missionaries and—"

Adam began to nod. "I know them well. I'll take you up to the Tillotson's home."

"You'll be better off there," Jed said, unable to meet her eyes. "With all this business about Indians, some folks feel kinda uncomfortable about you bein' here."

Elisabeth ignored the inference as her eyes moved toward the open door.

"Where is everyone?"

Jed kicked at a loose board. "Half the post left after your ma died and Carlotta—"

"We'll be leaving as soon as Elisabeth gets whatever she needs," Adam interrupted.

Jed merely grunted and stalked out.

Elisabeth stared after him. "How can anyone be so cruel?" she said dully, still unable to believe all that had happened.

"Elisabeth, he is an evil man. Sorry, but that's obvious to me. The sooner you're away from here, the better. Now let's pack your things."

She turned pain-filled eyes to him. "You're not evil. You're very good," she said, bewildered. "A stranger whom I've just met is kinder to me than a man I've called Father for all these years."

"There's a big difference, Elisabeth," he answered slowly. "I am a man of God."

seven

In a daze, Elisabeth opened her mother's trunk. More tears filled her eyes at the sight of the rumpled dresses, the sturdy work shoes, the heavy wool cloak.

Her hands scooped up the dresses, and she buried her face in the soft cloth, trying to find the lingering scent of her mother to forever etch in her memory. And it was there—the faint yeast-and-onion scent of Mary Greenwood.

Thank you, Ma, she thought. *Thanks for loving and caring for me. It couldn't have been easy. . .with him.* She quickly replaced the dresses, poking further into the trunk. Her fingers closed over a small object, loose among the dresses. She stared down at the cameo pin, lifting it gently to her lips. This was the treasure she sought, the one she would keep with pride.

She closed the lid and bundled up the last of her possessions in a clean flour sack from her mother's cupboard.

"I'm ready," she announced to Adam. Her face was pale, haunted, but her chin was set determinedly.

Elisabeth's eyes roamed over the cabin, silently bidding it good-bye. She hesitated in the door, remembering all the sessions with her tutor and the hopes and dreams of a bright future that she and her mother had shared. But the hand of fate had smashed those dreams, whisked away everything that had been comfortable and secure. She was alone now, with only her own ingenuity to shape her future, and already she could sense how difficult that future was going to be.

Adam had brought the horses to the door. It would save her the embarrassment of having to walk across the courtyard beneath the rude, appraising stares of those who had once been her friends but now stood in judgment of her. She tied her knapsack on the saddle, then climbed on her mare.

As Adam handed her the reins and walked around to his horse, Elisabeth held her head high and rode out of the post, never once looking back.

ﱞ

The afternoon stretched on as they rode in silence. Adam glanced worriedly at Elisabeth who hadn't spoken a word since they left the post. Her eyes were distant and haunted, and yet her mouth was set in a determined line. He knew she was hurting, but he chose to remain silent. She would have to come to terms with her pain, and that was going to take time.

He turned the leather reins over in his gloved hands, absently studying them. He was beginning to feel responsible for her, but he was certain she would manage all right once they arrived in Denver. The Tillotsons were good people. They had retired from the mission field and seemed to be content living in town.

"Where do you live?" she asked, breaking into his thoughts.

"I have a cabin in a mountain valley above Denver," he said, looking across at her. "I have a large circuit to cover, and my cabin is situated about halfway between the areas I travel."

She frowned. "You said you were fascinated by your uncle's stories. When did you know you wanted to do this kind of work?"

Adam considered her question. "Funny, it was always something I knew I wanted to do. As soon as I got saved—"

"Saved?" What was he talking about? "Saved from what?"

He smiled gently and began to tell her the story of the day his uncle had come to visit and taken him to church.

"Between listening to my uncle, then the pastor, my heart was touched. I knew I wanted to belong to this Jesus I heard about, and I wanted to do something worthwhile with my life. My uncle was the best role model I had ever met." He grinned. "I even live in his cabin." A sad expression touched his dark eyes. "He died soon after I came out here. It seemed natural that I would try to take his place in the world."

"I'm sure you must do a very good job," she said, looking deep into his eyes. "I can see you are a man of God; you've proven that to me. And I'd like to hear more about your faith. I had a tutor once who read to me from the Bible. I liked the sound of the words, but—"

"But what, Elisabeth?"

She sighed, turning her eyes toward the mountain peaks, jagged against the afternoon sky. "I'm going to have to settle some things in my mind before I can take on this God of yours."

"You've got it backwards," Adam said. "First you accept God, then you'll find that things get settled in your conscience."

She shook her head, puzzled. "You're confusing me."

He reached over and touched her hand. "I'll pray for you."

Her head whipped around to look at him. He was going to pray for her—no one had ever made such an offer before.

She smiled warmly. "Thank you."

"Now, do you mind if we stop at the Castleman's

boardinghouse just up the road at Lone Peak? Mrs. Castleman is very nice; I think you'll like her. We can't make it all the way to Denver today. I stop over at Mrs. Castleman's to break up the journey. Is that okay with you?"

Elisabeth shrugged. "Whatever you think."

Her thoughts were not on the boardinghouse or the trip to Denver; she was still thinking about this man who rode beside her and talked of being saved. The only kind of "saving" she understood at the moment was the way he had come into her life to save her from the horrible nightmare that faced her.

Elisabeth fell silent as the little community unfolded in a valley dominated by a jagged mountain peak. A row of rough pine buildings contained a mercantile, a saloon, a couple of eating establishments, and a stable and blacksmith shop. On the streets winding upward from main street she could see half a dozen log houses.

"We need to see to our horses first," Adam said, drawing rein at the log hitching rail before a large, open-ended building that was a combination of blacksmith shop and stable.

A heavyset man was laying a hot iron to a horseshoe, but at the sight of Adam, he plunged the iron into a barrel of water and came striding forward.

"Afternoon, Jake," Adam called.

Elisabeth looked at the man who was well over

six feet tall, with large, blunt features and shaggy gray hair. He shook hands with Adam, then glanced at Elisabeth and nodded politely.

"Jake, we'd like to leave our horses to be rubbed down. We've traveled quite a few miles. Thought we'd stop over at Mrs. Castleman's." He grinned. "Does she still make those good buckwheat pancakes?"

"They're better than ever." The big man rubbed his sagging stomach then reached over to stroke the neck of Adam's horse.

As Adam helped her down, Elisabeth felt as stiff as the board sidewalk beyond the blacksmith shop. She was unaccustomed to riding a horse so many miles, and every muscle in her body ached. Still, she didn't mind. She had started a new life, and she was beginning to feel hopeful again, now that she had met Adam Pearson.

"No use trying to go farther on an empty stomach," Adam said as they turned to cross the street. "And I could use a strong cup of coffee. What about you?"

"I suppose," Elisabeth replied, thinking of her ma's coffee and the kitchen in which she had grown up.

Swallowing hard, she tried to keep sad thoughts pushed back as they approached a large log house with a restaurant on one end. Passing under a hand-lettered sign that read "EATS," they entered the front door and were greeted by a cozy, cheerful room with red-checkered curtains at the window and half a dozen square tables and tall wooden chairs. Most of the people seated at the tables were men dressed in work clothes. Elisabeth dropped her eyes as Adam's hand touched her elbow protectively and guided her to a quiet table in the corner.

"Mrs. Castleman lost her husband to a mining accident two years ago. They had some money put back, which she used to fix up her place for boarding guests and an eating establishment."

A tiny brunette woman with a friendly smile approached their table and nodded in recognition as she looked at Adam.

"Well, hello! You've been a stranger to us lately."

"I haven't been in this area. Mrs. Castleman, this is Elisabeth Greenwood. I'm escorting her to Denver, but we need a couple of rooms tonight, if you have them."

The woman's little face registered her disappointment. "Sorry, Adam, but I only have one room, and it has to be shared with a Mrs. Martin from Denver."

Elisabeth's breath caught. *Now what?* she wondered.

"Then Elisabeth can take it, and I'll bunk over at the stable. It won't be the first time."

Elisabeth frowned across at him. "Are you sure?

I hate to—"

"He won't mind, dear," the little woman laid a hand on Elisabeth's arm. "This is the most agreeable fellow I've ever met. Now, you two must be hungry. What can I get for you?"

"Do you have any of those good buckwheat pancakes made up?"

"So happens I do." She grinned, wreathing her small face in a pleasant glow. "Two orders?"

He looked at Elisabeth. "Sound okay to you?"

"Sounds fine." She had no appetite, but she knew she must force herself to eat something to make the long journey to the Tillotson's house. Suddenly, she found herself thinking of her new life in Denver, and an unexpected feeling of excitement swept over her. Despite the tragedies she had faced, hope seemed to be building in her—perhaps it was having Adam's encouragement or maybe it was her own unstoppable optimism. Even in crises it seemed to surface as it did now.

"I'll get a job when we get to Denver," she said, thinking ahead.

Adam leaned back in the chair, appraising her thoughtfully. "What will you do?"

She hesitated. "I guess I'll find a job cooking. I know how to do that. Or maybe I could be a chambermaid at one of the hotels."

Adam nodded, studying his hands. Elisabeth

sensed he was worried about something. "What's wrong?"

"Oh, nothing." A smile touched his lips, and Elisabeth found herself thinking of how handsome he was—so tall and masculine, yet he spoke in a gentle manner, and as far as she could tell, he seemed to possess a heart of gold.

"Well, actually, I suppose I should warn you, there are lots of women looking for work, and many of the jobs are taken."

Elisabeth frowned. "Where do the women come from?"

"Miners' wives whose husbands spend all their time up in the hills panning the streams or trapping in the woods. So many people flooded into the territory when gold was discovered at Cherry Creek. Frankly, I think that supply has been exhausted. Now they're having to range farther. Money is scarce, and most wives don't see their husbands for weeks, or sometimes months."

"That doesn't sound like a very good life for those women." But then she thought of her mother and a pang of sadness touched her heart. "It's the way things are, I guess. All women have to work hard now," she said in a deep sigh.

The pancakes arrived, huge round cakes drizzled with butter and honey, and Elisabeth's mouth watered. Maybe she was hungrier than she thought.

They fell silent as they began to eat, then Elisabeth asked the question that had been puzzling her for the past hour. "How long will you be in Denver?"

"Just long enough to get you settled, check in with my home church, rest a day or so, then head out again."

"Oh,. And how long are you out on your circuit?"

"Well," he lifted his fork and speared into a huge pancake, "I'll be out a long time. I only come into Denver a few times a year to buy supplies and meet with my mission board. The rest of the time, I use my cabin as headquarters and branch out across the back side of the Rockies."

Elisabeth stared at him. "I guess it's a miracle we met."

A tiny smile lit his dark eyes. "Honestly, it is. I came to your post for the first time the other day when I had to make a trip down to Colorado City to meet with another missionary. I like to compare their method of witnessing and delivering Bibles to the way we do things up here. Also, they have news from other mission posts. I do stop in at Lone Eagle's camp when I'm on that road. I'm hoping soon to deliver some Bibles to them and try to teach them something about the Word of God."

The pancake grew heavy in her mouth as Elisabeth stared at him, trying to imagine him out doing this kind of work. It was so different from anything she had ever heard about. "Do you plan to keep doing this. . .this mission work for the rest of your life?"

His eyes drifted slowly over her features, and she wondered what he was thinking. "Always," he said with conviction.

"Oh." She tried to suppress the sigh forming in her chest. He was such a kind, likeable man. Why couldn't he be a merchant, or do some kind of work in Denver? That way maybe there would be a chance she could see him more often. But with his job, she knew she would rarely see him, and she found herself growing oddly sad.

"You'll like being with the Tillotsons," he said, shifting in his chair and looking around the room. "They're a very nice older couple. Since he retired, though, his health has not been good. I think the cold winters make him worse. They've talked of going south, but I don't think they plan to do that yet."

"Well," Elisabeth said hastily, "I don't want to be any trouble to them. As soon as I get a job, I can move into a boardinghouse like this one."

Adam nodded, yet there was a small frown gathering between his brows. Elisabeth wondered what he was thinking.

❧

It was good she couldn't read his thoughts for they were troubled. Jobs, like inexpensive rooms, were scarce in Denver. She was a beautiful woman who was going to attract a lot of men, and he greatly feared what could happen to such an innocent girl in this restless city.

He dropped his eyes to his pancakes and tried not to think about that now. His responsibility was to get her to the Tillotsons, then pray that she could make a new life in Denver.

A heavy feeling tugged at his heart. He was afraid he was going to have a hard time riding off, forgetting her. Already, there were strong feelings for this woman churning in his heart, although he didn't see how there could be a future for them. He couldn't expect a woman to share his rough life, and he could sense that Elisabeth didn't have the same faith in God that he did.

As he pushed his empty plate aside and sipped at his coffee, he knew tonight's prayers would last longer than usual.

eight

Elisabeth's room was comfortable, even with only the bare necessities—two iron cots, two washstands, a couple of chairs, and a small rag rug that covered less than three square feet of the cold plank floor. She shared the room with an older woman who slept with her mouth open.

Elisabeth tossed and turned on her cot throughout the night, listening to Mrs. Martin's snores. It had been a relief when finally the morning sunlight slipped into the room and Mrs. Martin roused from her bed.

She was a matronly type, in her forties, whose gray eyes were filled with despair as she related her life's story to Elisabeth.

"We never should have left Texas! But Harold swore he'd strike it rich if we could just sell our little spread and join the wagon train heading to Pike's Peak." Tears welled in her eyes. "We've spent most of our money, and now Harold's living up in the mountains like an animal, waiting for the weather to break so he can strike it rich." She shook her head, her eyes betraying her bitterness. "We never should have left Texas!"

Elisabeth took a deep breath, trying to think how to console her. "Maybe your husband will find some gold this time."

The woman continued shaking her head miserably. "Either a fellow's lucky or he's not. My Harold's been unlucky all his life." The corners of her mouth sagged downward in a perpetual expression of defeat.

As Elisabeth looked at the woman, she felt a rush of pity for her. Were these the kind of people Adam was witnessing to up in the mountains and back country? If so, he was doing a wonderful work, for Elisabeth didn't think she'd ever seen anyone look so miserable. She tried to think what she could say to help. She thought about what the woman had said about her husband's bad "luck." It was a silly word. She wished she knew what kind of advice Adam would offer, so that she could speak the right words now to this woman who desperately needed hope and encouragement.

She remembered what Adam had said to her; the words had almost instantly made her feel better. She took a breath and looked at Mrs. Martin.

"I'll pray for you," Elisabeth said, although she wasn't certain what such a prayer would hold.

The woman looked startled, then she began to smile as she dabbed at her eyes with a worn handkerchief. "Thank you, dear. I know God can help; He is the *only* one who can help us now."

۶

Elisabeth had changed into a long-sleeved, dark-print dress, hoping it would be fashionable enough for Denver. Winding her long hair into a braided chignon, she inserted the hairpins carefully, studying the dark eyes that peered at her through the looking glass.

For no reason she could think of, she was remembering the pain and agony she had seen in Morning Dove's dark eyes and the suffering she had endured.

Elisabeth closed her eyes, willing her mind to shut off the memory. She had done what she could to help; now she must put the experience out of her thoughts. They had a made a mistake, that was all. Even though her eyes and hair were dark, her skin was too light, her features too small. She was *not* the daughter of an Indian woman, she was certain of that.

Thinking she had put the matter to rest, she thrust her feet in her kid boots and went downstairs to meet Adam.

۶

"Good morning," he called to her. He was waiting in the front hall, dressed in a clean flannel shirt and tan trousers. His thick dark hair was neatly combed, and his brown eyes glowed as he watched her approach.

"Good morning." She smiled up at him.

Her eyes locked with his for a moment before he cleared his throat and looked around.

"Hungry?" he asked.

She shrugged. "No. Look, Adam, about the expense money—"

"I am allowed expense money in my missionary work. You can repay me once you get a job in Denver."

She frowned. "I don't know how long that will be." She had thought of something the night before, however, and she was quick to share the idea with Adam. "Once we get to Denver, will you help me sell my mare?"

Adam looked surprised. "Won't you need to keep her?"

She shook her head. "I can get another horse later on, and I need the money. Please, Adam, will you help me?"

He nodded thoughtfully. "If that's what you want to do. She's a stout little mare, and I'm certain we won't have any trouble finding a buyer. A good horse is always in demand."

Elisabeth breathed a sigh of relief, feeling a bit more independent. Now she didn't feel so bad about taking money from him. *It's only a temporary loan until we reach Denver,* she told herself.

"Let's not worry anymore. Try to relax and let's

get some breakfast."

Elisabeth nodded, realizing she was beginning to depend on Adam too much. And yet there was more than dependence involved. She had feelings for Adam; she had felt something the very first time she saw him at the post—she had to squelch those feelings.

Elisabeth forced herself to look toward Mrs. Castleman, who was entering the front door. She needed to thank her for her kindness and then say good-bye. She had a new life in Denver to think about.

٭

As they rode toward Denver, Elisabeth enjoyed the view of sweeping mountains and open valleys. Occasionally, an antelope or deer bounded across the meadow or darted daringly in front of them. Her mind drifted back to the post and the years she had spent there. It seemed like another lifetime, and not a happy one.

They stopped for lunch at the home of a farmer whose wife served travelers as a means of helping with their income, or so Adam had told her. They dined on fried venison, creamed potatoes, and thick gravy in large bowls on one long table.

Two older men, traveling together, sat across from Elisabeth and Adam.

"What's going on in the outside world?" Adam

asked conversationally.

"The war down south's heating up," one man complained.

A deep frown knitted Adam's dark brows. "Do you think it will end anytime soon?"

"Don't know what will happen," the man answered. "But Governor Gilpin's letting too many deserters into our territory."

"What do you think of our governor?" Adam asked, looking from one man to the other.

"Gilpin's supposed to be an expert when it comes to civil government. He's already touring the mining camps, taking a census of the population of the Colorado Territory. There'll be an election to choose delegates to Congress and the legislature."

"We're getting too civilized," the other man grumbled, taking a deep sip of coffee.

"There's been more trouble between the Utes and Arapahoes," the more congenial man continued, undaunted by his friend's gruffness. "And the Cheyenne are giving newcomers out on the plains a hard time."

"I've yet to meet an Indian that wasn't a savage," the grumpy man put in.

"Oh, I don't agree," Adam drawled. "I travel around the territory, visiting some of the camps. They've always been good to me. But maybe that's because I'm part Indian myself."

A tense silence fell over the group. Elisabeth leapt to her feet.

"I'd like to go," she said quickly, glancing at the men, who were watching Adam, then her. Were they looking at her at bit differently too? Did she look like a half-breed? *Was she?*

Her arm swept out, carelessly knocking her water glass to the floor. At the sound of broken glass, the farmer's wife scurried out of the kitchen with a broom and a dustpan.

"I'm so sorry," Elisabeth mumbled, feeling the blood rush to her cheeks. She glanced desperately at Adam.

"Could we pay for the glass?"

"Isn't necessary," the woman replied, busily sweeping up the shards of glass.

"I am sorry," Elisabeth said in a rush, then hurried out the door.

Outside, she breathed deeply of the crisp cold air, wondering what on earth had come over her. She was acting ridiculous, behaving as though she felt guilty about something.

She heard the door close as Adam rushed to her side. "Why are you acting this way?" For the first time, Adam's tone held an edge of irritation.

"I can't help it. Their talk of savages!"

"Then, why not defend those *savages,* rather than run from the truth?"

She whirled around, glaring up at him. "And what do you consider the truth?"

He shrugged. "Does it matter? You're being unfair, not giving the Indians a fair chance to—"

"To what? Kidnap me again?" She turned and charged toward her horse. "Don't try defending them to me, Adam Pearson. Because of those savages, my mother is dead!"

Adam's expression changed from one of irritation to something more unreadable. He said nothing more as he strode to his horse and untied the reins, leaving her to do the same.

As she scrambled back into the saddle, she began to regret her harsh words with him. He was kindest person she had ever met. But why did he have to be such a goody-goody, always defending the Indians?

But then, of course, he was half Cherokee himself. And he was proud, not ashamed. Closing her eyes for a moment, she tried to think of a way to bridge the awkward gap. She had spoken too quickly, and she had probably offended him, as well. She cleared her throat, trying to soften her tone of voice. "I'm just anxious to get to Denver, aren't you?"

He hesitated for a moment. "Very anxious."

"At least you'll be rid of me," she said, testing his mood with a little smile.

He didn't smile back. He merely turned his horse up the road, and Elisabeth decided he wasn't the "goody-goody" she had thought him to be. He was a kind man, but it was obvious that he had a temper when someone offended him or the people he held dear.

Maybe that was not a bad thing. She sighed, realizing there was no one in her life left to defend. Her mother was dead. *Maybe both of your mothers are dead,* a thought whispered in the back of her brain.

≈

As they rode in silence for the next half hour, she dared not look at him. She couldn't help how she had reacted. It had been a traumatic week for her. Still she had to get ahold of herself. The Utes had made a mistake, that was all; she was not one of them, she had no feelings of love for them.

She knew she should apologize for being so rude, but she couldn't seem to find the right words. She was glad he wasn't talking to her; she didn't want to talk to him either.

She focused her eyes on the melting snowbanks that lined the sides of the road. She would be glad to get to Denver.

≈

It was early afternoon when Elisabeth first saw the sprawling settlement of Denver, built out in the flats with the jagged, frost-glistened peaks of the front range as a backdrop. The mountains had given way to hills with table-flat summits and sandstone ridges as the country opened up, stretching out before them.

"That's Cherry Creek," Adam said, pointing to a narrow stream threading its way between two rows of cabins built of cottonwood logs and roofed with earth and grass. "It used to be the dividing line between Aurora and Denver. Folks fussed and occasionally fought each other for the miners' and settlers' trade. Finally they realized that the only way either could succeed was to join forces as one town: Denver City."

She took a deep breath, relieved that he seemed to have gotten over his irritation with her.

"You seem to know a lot about the area," she said, eager for a safe topic of conversation.

"My uncle lived in Denver when it was first being settled. He said it was like one giant ant heap. People were crowded into tents and crude shacks, even sleeping under wagons. Half of them were ready to turn around and head home. But they stayed and built this town, and now many are successful merchants. The only problem is," he turned his reins over in his hands, "they seem to have forgotten the years when they had to do without; otherwise, I don't know how they could charge as much as fifteen dollars for a sack of flour. That's what I paid when I stocked up for my trip home."

Home. The word was like manna to her ears, and

suddenly, more than anything, she wanted a home of her own.

"Tell me about where you live." She looked across at him.

He turned his face toward the mountains, and she could see that the subject pleased him. A smile tilted his lips, stretching to the creases in his cheeks.

"My cabin is on a stream on the back side of a mountain. Only a few cabins are scattered about in the small area called Aspen Valley."

"That's a pretty name," Elisabeth said, studying the log buildings they passed. "I suppose the aspens are pretty there in the fall."

"A beauty that takes your breath away," he said. "Well, here we are."

She was sorry they had stopped talking about his cabin. It sounded so peaceful and homey. But it was time to think about the Tillotsons and her new life here in Denver. She studied the brightly lettered signs over the doors of shops and on the sides of buildings. There was a gun shop, a carpenter shop, a hardware store that boasted stoves made of sheet iron, a meat market, bakery, saloon and gambling hall, and barber shop. Graham's Drug Store offered watches and jewelry made to order from native gold.

"This is quite a town," she said, looking around and feeling a bit lost and out of place.

"It's fine if you like towns, I guess. We'll take this next street to the right. The Tillotsons live down at the end."

Elisabeth nodded, trying to force her mind toward what she would say to them. She hated to tell them why she was here, perhaps it wouldn't be necessary to tell them everything. She could say that her mother had died, but before her death, she had sent her to look up the Tillotsons.

It had been a long time since she'd seen the older couple. Perhaps they wouldn't even want her to stay with them. She glanced across at Adam's strong yet gentle features. She would never forget Adam; she had never met anyone quite like him. And rather than think of the Tillotsons, she found herself thinking of Adam. Again.

nine

The Tillotsons lived in a small frame house located in a nice neighborhood and within walking distance of the shops. Elisabeth decided it would be a perfect place for her as they turned their horses in at the hitching rail near the front gate. The small patch of yard was covered with snow, but the little porch had been swept clean. White lace curtains fluttered at the windows, offering a cozy invitation. It had the look of home to Elisabeth, and she was desperate for one.

Almost as soon as Adam knocked, the door swung open, and Mrs. Tillotson, a tiny birdlike woman, surveyed them beneath thick white hair and wire spectacles.

"Hello, Mrs. Tillotson." Adam extended his hand.

"Adam! How good to see you. And I know we have met," she looked at Elisabeth, "but I'm having trouble remembering exactly when."

"I'm Jed. . .and Mary Greenwood's daughter," she stumbled over those words, then hurried on. "When you were at the trading post—"

"Of course! I would have recognized you instantly

if I had seen you in that area. Just wasn't expecting you in Denver. It's good to see you, my dear."

"It's nice to see you," Elisabeth said, shaking her hand.

"Please! Come inside and let me make a pot of tea. You two must be half-frozen. It's such a cold day."

The little woman bustled ahead of them, down a narrow hallway, motioning them to a room off to the right. "Go into the parlor and warm yourselves, I have a fire going. I'll get that tea."

As they entered the small room and looked around, Elisabeth saw that it was filled with touches of home and family. Framed photographs of a man and woman dominated tables covered with crocheted doilies; needlepoint pillows graced the sofa, and sturdy rocking chairs were drawn near a cozy fire in a small hearth.

Adam looked around. "Mr. Tillotson must be out. Let's have a seat." He motioned her to the nearest chair.

As Elisabeth took a seat, enjoying the cheery fire, Mrs. Tillotson bustled back, carrying a tray with a china teapot and cups. "Luckily, I already had the kettle going so there's no wait," she called over her shoulder.

"We'll be glad to get some tea," Adam replied. "How is Mr. Tillotson?"

Turning to face them, the older woman's smile gave way to a terrible sadness as she put the tray on a table and sighed. "You don't know, of course. He passed away a couple weeks ago."

Adam went to her side, hugging her gently. "No, I didn't know. I'm so sorry to hear that. He was a wonderful man."

"Yes, he was," she sniffed, reaching into her apron pocket for a lace handkerchief. "We never had children and I'm so lonely. But he died suddenly. I'm thankful for that." She dabbed at her eyes and looked across at Elisabeth. "Young lady, what brings you to Denver?"

Elisabeth hesitated, looking at Adam.

"Could we get some of that hot tea first, Mrs. Tillotson?" Adam intervened.

"Oh, of course." She turned to fill the cups.

As she poured tea, Elisabeth tried to explain that her mother had passed away, and that before she died she told Elisabeth to come to Denver. "I plan to get a job here and—"

"Then, you must stay with me! I have a spare bedroom, and I need the company. I miss my husband awfully. You must miss your mother too. She was a good woman."

Elisabeth nodded, sipping her tea to ward off the tightness that clutched at her throat. She was aware of both Adam and Mrs. Tillotson watching her thoughtfully, and she couldn't bear the thought of breaking into tears in front of them. Clearing her throat, she tried to think of the practical matters involved in living with Mrs. Tillotson.

"Mrs. Tillotson," she said, "I expect to pay for my room and board."

"We'll see about that."

"Please. It's the only way I'll feel comfortable about staying."

The little lady lifted her shoulders in a light shrug. "Well, since you put it that way. . . But only after you're settled into a job." She looked at Adam. "How is the mission field?"

He sighed. "Busier than ever. There are so many to reach, so much territory to cover—"

"You can't do it all. It's an impossible task. Which is why our missionary society has launched a campaign to get some outposts established. Aspen Valley is on our list."

"Is that right?" Adam smiled politely.

"Yes. It's only your youth and enthusiasm that allows you to cover so much territory, and we know there are many trappers and traders back there who need a church. And the Indians desperately need to hear the Word of God."

Adam looked across at Elisabeth, who dropped her eyes.

"Are you two hungry?" Mrs. Tillotson asked suddenly.

"Oh no," Elisabeth replied, glancing at Adam.

"Actually, we have business to take care of. We're going to the livery to sell Elisabeth's mare. Then I have to be on my way home."

Elisabeth felt her heart sink upon hearing those words. She hated the thought of Adam leaving, but she knew there was nothing she could do about it. She felt guilty for taking up so much of his time, when Mrs. Tillotson had just pointed out how busy he was.

"You'll stay for supper, won't you? I won't hear of you riding back into the wilds on an empty stomach."

"Since you put it that way," he grinned, "I will be pleased to stay for one of your good meals. Then I'll be on my way."

❧

The day passed all too quickly, for the knowledge that Adam was leaving lay heavy on Elisabeth's mind. He had obtained a good price for her mare and instructed her how to best stretch her money until she found work. Then they sat down to a tasty meal with Mrs. Tillotson. It was obvious that the tiny widow had missed having conversations with someone, for she began to talk as soon as she served them.

"I wish that crazy war down south hadn't started,"

Mrs. Tillotson complained. "Are you worried about your family down there, Adam?"

Adam sighed and nodded slowly, staring at his cup. "My father is still in east Tennessee."

Elisabeth stared at Adam, sensing his concern.

"Bless you," Mrs. Tillotson leaned forward, laying a small hand on his arm. "When did you last hear from your family?"

"I haven't heard from my father in years. I write him but he rarely answers." He took a deep breath and turned sad eyes to Mrs. Tillotson. "He wanted me to stay in the South, but my calling was in the West."

Mrs. Tillotson was wiggling in her seat, her concern obvious. "Do you think he might get involved in this awful mess?"

"His health is poor and we have no family. I doubt that he will leave his farm if it's possible for him to stay there."

Mrs. Tillotson nodded and sighed. Then something else seemed to occur to her. "Don't you think men are warriors at heart, Adam?"

Elisabeth watched Adam grin at her and speak pleasantly, even though some men would take offense at such a question.

"Now, why do you say that, Mrs. Tillotson?"

"I'm not talking about you, of course, or my husband, God rest his soul. It just seems that so many men have to have a gun or tomahawk in their hands and drive their horses into battle. I think it goes back to something primal in our bloodline when warriors sat before the fire each evening discussing their victories and their losses."

Elisabeth's glance slid from Adam to Mrs. Tillotson then back to the vegetables on her plate. Each time the word *tomahawk* was mentioned, she found herself shifting or twisting or feeling uncomfortable. She had to stop acting this way. Adam was half Cherokee and he didn't seem to take offense.

"About the war," Adam spoke up, "I never agreed with slavery. I'm afraid the South is in for some hard times because a lot of people are resisting change. But it's too bad that there has to be a war to settle the differences between North and South."

"It's just terrible." Mrs. Tillotson shook her head.

"Well," Adam was rising from the table, "I really must get started. I have a long ride ahead. Mrs. Tillotson, I'm grateful for your wonderful meal."

"You're more than welcome, Adam," she said as her eyes moved to Elisabeth. "And I'm grateful for my new companion."

"I'll say good evening, then."

"I'll walk with you." Elisabeth stood quickly, hating the thought of saying good-bye.

"I appreciate all you've done," she said as they walked out the front door. "You rescued me at the Ute camp, you took me to the post, and now you've brought me here. And thanks for selling my mare." As she looked up at him, she felt a ridiculous urge to burst into tears.

"I've enjoyed being with you, Elisabeth. And I'll be praying for you."

"I'll need your prayers," she forced a smile, "but I'll be fine here." She looked up at the sky where only the pale sickle moon rested against the clouds. "It's an awful dark night for you to be riding back."

"I'll be fine."

"Again, Adam, I don't know how to thank you," Elisabeth said, as they reached the hitching rail and he began to untie his horse.

"No thanks are necessary. On second thought," he turned back to her, "there is something you can do for me."

Elisabeth was puzzled. He had never asked anything from her.

"What is it?"

"I want you to try and resolve who you are. It doesn't really matter who your earthly parents are. We all have the same Father, the same loving God. There's a verse in the Bible that I sometimes give to the people who call on me for advice when they are having financial or family problems. I give them Matthew 6:33, 'Seek ye first the kingdom of God, and his righteousness; and all these things shall be added unto you'."

She nodded thoughtfully. "So you're saying when I accept God I will have my heritage."

"That's what I'm trying to say."

He couldn't really understand what she was going through. No one could. But she knew he meant well.

"You are a very special, lady, Elisabeth." Their eyes locked, and he seemed to read the conflict that raged within her. He turned to leave, saying no more.

Her hand shot to his arm, touching his sleeve lightly. "Have a safe trip back."

He nodded, gripping her hand. Then, as if on impulse, he lowered his head and kissed her gently.

Elisabeth's senses reeled. This was her first kiss, and she had never felt anything like the tenderness and gentleness that was Adam. When he drew back from her and their dark eyes met in the sparse moonlight, she felt her heart beating faster.

"I must go," Adam said, pulling up into the saddle.

Nodding, she waved to him and watched him ride off into the night. Then, as he disappeared, a terrible loneliness swept over her. It was only then that she began to realize she had fallen in love with Adam.

ten

As Elisabeth sat at the kitchen table, having coffee with Mrs. Tillotson, she related her frustration over not having found a job.

"Well," Mrs. Tillotson was thoughtful, "I don't know if this would interest you, but there's a new photographer in town. He's set up shop in that little building next to the newspaper office. He has no help. Why don't you talk to him?"

"That's a good idea. Thanks for mentioning it, Mrs. Tillotson."

Photographer. How interesting. She couldn't wait to go and speak with him about a job. So far there was nothing available in the hotels or restaurants where she had tried. Adam had been right; many women had gotten in line ahead of her to get a job, and most jobs available were already taken. She had been looking for over a week now, but she tried to hide her discouragement from Mrs. Tillotson, who had been so encouraging.

"I'll go today," Elisabeth said, finishing her tea.

⸾

Elisabeth located the *Gallery*, as the sign read, and

quickly decided to work for whatever he could pay
her if he would just hire her. She needed the money;
furthermore, she needed something to occupy her
mind. Added to her sadness over her mother's death
was the sharp ache of missing Adam, much more
than she had dreamed possible.

She stood for a moment before the false-front
shop, taking a deep breath. She'd never had any
experience at this sort of work, and for a moment
she felt rather foolish. Just then a funny little man
opened the door. He was small, with brown eyes
and hair, and a long nose above a handlebar moustache.

"Come in," he said, looking eager for business.

Elisabeth acknowledged his invitation and entered,
glancing about at the cozy front room. An exhibit of
photographs covered the wall. Elisabeth thought
they were very pretty as she looked at views of
mountains, miners at work, and for contrast, a busy
Eastern city.

"You do nice work," she said, glancing at him.

"Thank you! Allow me to introduce myself. I'm
Seth Wilkerson from New York."

Elisabeth's eyes took in his slim small frame—he
was no more than an inch or two taller than she,
which seemed quite short in comparison to Adam.
In his thirties, Seth was dressed in a dark suit, obviously tailor-made, because it fit him to perfection.

"How do you do. I'm Elisabeth Greenwood." She extended a gloved hand.

"You'll make a lovely photograph! I'd be most eager—"

"Excuse me, but I stopped in to see if you need someone to work for you." At his shocked expression, she glanced around the room, trying to think how to win him over. "Where do you make the pictures?" she asked.

"In here," he said, opening a door. "There's a tiny dressing room back there, the room just off the parlor, and this is my laboratory."

Through the open door, Elisabeth could see a darkroom covered with orange cloth.

"I use orange light because it doesn't harm my glass plates," he explained.

"I see." Elisabeth nodded. "You have some expensive-looking equipment here. It seems to me you need someone to watch your gallery if you have to be away."

"Well. . .yes, I do. I've been wanting to make another trip to the mining camps to get pictures of the miners. They love to send photographs home to show their families, displaying their working situations."

"Then I could take care of your gallery while you're away. I could keep the place clean, make tea for your customers."

"Yes. . .I suppose I do need a helper. . .but the wages would be very small in the beginning."

"It doesn't matter." She smiled. "I want a job. Do you know Mrs. Marjorie Tillotson? I live with her."

"Mrs. Tillotson?" His eyebrow hiked and his smile widened. "She's a lovely lady. We attend the same church." He withdrew a gold watch from his vest pocket, glanced at the time, then returned it to his pocket. "Miss Greenwood, I'm due at the bank for a meeting. You can start to work right now. If anyone comes for a photograph, don't let them leave until I return!"

Elisabeth's mouth fell open as he grabbed his hat and sailed out the door. Then, smiling after him, she removed her cloak and gloves and looked around. There was a thin layer of dust on the board floor so she went in search of a broom.

&

That evening as she sat with Mrs. Tillotson, she let the older woman serve her tea and chat about a benefit cake sale the Ladies' Missionary Society was planning, but Elisabeth scarcely heard a word. She was thinking about Adam, and feeling amazed that she missed him so much.

A knock on the door interrupted Mrs. Tillotson's constant flow of words, and she cocked her little head to one side, obviously startled.

"Now, who on earth would be calling at this

hour?" She looked at Elisabeth, who found herself hoping that Adam had returned.

Mrs. Tillotson peered through the curtains and then gave a little cry of delight. "It's Star of the Morning!"

"Star of the Morning?" Elisabeth repeated, puzzled, as Mrs. Tillotson rushed for the door and quickly turned the key in the lock. "Star of the Morning, what a pleasant surprise! Do come in." Mrs. Tillotson opened the door.

Elisabeth watched a beautiful young woman, dressed in a white doeskin dress and matching moccasins, enter the room. Her hair was jet black, as were her eyes, and her skin a smooth olive. She had small, pretty features, and her clothes were immaculate. Elisabeth's breath caught. She was the prettiest Indian woman she had ever seen.

"Hello." She smiled at Mrs. Tillotson then looked toward Elisabeth, a question in her eyes.

"Dear, this is Elisabeth Greenwood," Mrs. Tillotson said, laying a hand on Star of the Morning's fringed sleeve.

"Hello." Elisabeth smiled back at her, her mind filled with questions.

"Hello, Elisabeth." The young Indian woman looked about Elisabeth's age and spoke English perfectly.

"Elisabeth, Star of the Morning was our best pupil

at the mission school."

Elisabeth smiled. "Congratulations."

"Elisabeth is from down in the Pike's Peak region," Mrs. Tillotson continued. "Her folks have a trading post there. I'm sure her father traded with your people."

Elisabeth almost choked at those words, knowing how, given the chance, Jed Greenwood had swindled everyone who came through his door.

"I want to go to that area." Star of the Morning smiled. "I am hoping to be sent there to help my people."

"Star of the Morning is Ute and has a calling to return to teach. She has now completed her education." Mrs. Tillotson gave her a hug. "We're so proud of her."

"It has taken your prayers and your help." Star of the Morning returned Mrs. Tillotson's embrace.

Elisabeth was at a loss for words. This young woman was so pretty, so vibrant, and certainly seemed to be led by God. Elisabeth fell silent, not knowing what more she should say. Her mind whirled back to the time she had spent in Lone Eagle's camp and the kind people she had met there. In retrospect, she knew she had never given them a chance, for she had made up her mind that these were not her people, and all she could think about at the time was leaving.

Mrs. Tillotson was busily seeing to her guest. "Here, dear, take a seat. Have you eaten?"

"Yes, thank you." Star of the Morning settled gracefully onto the sofa, tucking her moccasined feet together at the ankles.

"Then, I'll make tea. I'm sure you could drink a cup of tea."

"That would be nice." She smiled gratefully at Mrs. Tillotson.

As the older woman hurried off for tea, Elisabeth couldn't help staring at the pretty girl, who appeared to be near her own age, opposite her.

"What brings you to Denver?" Star of the Morning asked pleasantly. Her dark eyes glowed in her smooth face as she looked across at Elisabeth.

"Well. . ." she began, then hesitated. Why try to pretend? Something about this woman evoked honesty, and she felt much the same way she had when she first met Adam in that she could tell her the truth.

"If I am being too personal, you do not have to answer." Star of the Morning seemed to sense a problem.

"No, I was just thinking how to phrase this." Elisabeth glanced over her shoulder toward the kitchen. "It's a long story. There was a. . .misunderstanding with my adoptive father after my mother died. My mother was a good woman, and she wanted me to come to Denver if anything happened." Her voice trailed as she felt grief welling up in her throat.

Star of the Morning began to nod. "I see. Then you could not choose a better home or a better person than Mrs. Tillotson. When I first came here to the mission school, she was my sponsor. I was a skinny frightened little thing," she laughed softly, "and Mrs. Tillotson and the other ladies at the mission school were so good to me. They changed my life." She hesitated, studying her slim graceful fingers. "My parents were killed in a battle out on the plains. That was my home. I had nowhere to go, and my people were starving. The Tillotsons were missionaries at the time; they came to our village and brought some of the children back here to the mission school. They saved our lives, and I will always be grateful."

As her soft voice trailed into silence, Elisabeth nodded, seeing how her life had been shaped for her missionary work. "You seem to have made the most of a difficult situation. I respect that."

"Here we are, girls." Mrs. Tillotson hurried back, bearing her tray of tea cups and teapot, steaming with the aroma of fresh herbed tea. "This will warm us up a bit on a cold winter night."

As she poured tea, Mrs. Tillotson began to pelt Star of the Morning with questions concerning the mission school. The young woman answered each question, patiently and competently, as they sipped their tea. Elisabeth felt herself relaxing, enjoying the evening, and she realized this was largely due to Star of the Morning's radiant presence.

As they finished their tea, Star of the Morning put down her cup and stood. "I must go now. I only came to say hello. I have to get back to the school. I am preparing to leave at the end of the week."

"Must you go?" Mrs. Tillotson looked distressed. "Where are they sending you?"

"That I do not know," she smiled, "but it doesn't matter. God is with me; I will go where I am needed."

Mrs. Tillotson hugged her affectionately. "Bless you, my child. You are such a credit to your nation."

At those words, Elisabeth felt as though her heart were shrinking. She was torn with embarrassment because she had not worked toward being a credit to anyone—white or Indian. Seeing the way Star of the Morning had turned her adversity around to make her life count for a good cause, Elisabeth felt a wave of shame sweeping over her. When she thought she was linked to the Ute tribe, she had been appalled and embarrassed, and now she was sorry for the way she had felt. She wanted to change those feelings, and yet she couldn't seem to do that on her own.

"It was nice meeting you, Elisabeth," Star of the Morning was saying. "Maybe I'll see you again."

"I hope so." Elisabeth smiled at her. And she did hope that their paths would cross again. She was more impressed with Star of the Morning than anyone she had met.

Except for Adam.

eleven

The next day Elisabeth had a few minutes of spare time before going to work, and she sauntered into the mercantile store. Women shopping there were dressed in fine woolens and dainty bonnets. Patent leather gaiters peeped from beneath their crinolines. She tried not to stare, but she couldn't help wishing she did not feel so out of place in her old-fashioned cotton dress.

As she looked around, her eyes nearly popped at the endless array of items labeled *Pike's Peak*. There were Pike's Peak guns, shovels and picks, Pike's Peak boots and hats. An outfit displayed with a small sign proclaiming it to be the "New American Costume" was made of dark calico with a knee-length skirt from which peeped a pair of matching pantalets.

Amused by it, Elisabeth stared for a moment then wandered toward a long woolen dress, blue as a Colorado sky. She trailed her fingers over the soft nubby cloth, wishing she could afford such a dress. Now that she had a job, she could use some of the money from the sale of her mare. Did she dare?

Her mind automatically raced to Adam. She would like to wear a dress like that when he returned. She wanted to style her hair, fix herself up pretty for him.

She tried to dredge up her logic, be rational, but she kept thinking about Adam, and impulsively, she walked over to the counter. "I'd like to try that one on, please." She pointed toward the blue dress.

"Certainly," the older woman smiled. "There's a dressing room right back there."

Elisabeth dashed behind a curtain and changed into the soft blue dress. The tucked bodice molded to her tiny waist then swirled in a perfect circle around her feet. She stared into the looking glass. The soft blue accented the darkness of her eyes and hair. As she stared at herself, an odd thought struck her: she did not look so different from Star of the Morning. Her hair had the same dark radiance, her eyes. . .

She dropped her head. It was true, she knew it was. She really did possess Ute blood. Drained of her enthusiasm, she removed the dress and changed back into her faded clothes. Gingerly, she carried it back outside to hang it up again.

"That color must be stunning on you." The helpful saleslady rushed up, obviously hoping for a sale.

"It's a very pretty dress," Elisabeth sighed. "I

need to think about it."

"Don't think long," she replied, taking the dress from Elisabeth to rehang. "We just got it in, and I daresay it won't stay here long."

Elisabeth nodded. "Thank you." She walked out the door and headed to work, her thoughts whirling. What if it was true? What is she was Ute? Was that so bad, after all?

Confusion filled her mind like a winter fog. She had to think about her job, she had to get her mind on what she was doing.

Her steps quickened as she hurried to work, glancing around her at the people crowding the sidewalks some of the men were dressed in red shirts and buckskins, others in dark business suits. It was exciting to live in a busy town, in one sense; but she missed the wide-open views and fresh air of her home. She thought of Star of the Morning and then, of course, Adam.

She wondered about the place he lived. She must remember to ask Mrs. Tillotson more about him.

As she turned into the shop, she saw that her new employer was busily packing up his supplies.

"Since you can stay here today, I'm going into the mountains," he announced, carefully loading a camera into its case.

"I'll take good care of things," she offered, removing her cloak and smoothing her cotton dress.

Automatically, she headed for the broom closet to tidy up the shop.

❧

That evening she sat before the fire with Mrs. Tillotson, listening to more news of the benefit cake sale that the Ladies' Missionary Society was planning.

When the little woman had finally run down, Elisabeth ventured a few questions about Adam.

"He is a wonderful young man, don't you think?" Mrs. Tillotson asked, cocking her little white head to one side and studying Elisabeth thoughtfully.

"He is nice. And he seems dedicated to his mission work here."

"Yes, he is." She looked into space, remembering. "His mother was a Cherokee in Tennessee. He has a calling to help all Indians."

Elisabeth dropped her eyes. She had not told Mrs. Tillotson the full story of her life. She was waiting for the right moment or for a time when she had settled the issue in her heart.

"Adam has done so many kind things for his people."

"Tell me about the area where he lives." Elisabeth slipped to the edge of her seat, as if anxious to hear about him.

Studying her, Mrs. Tillotson smiled and began to explain what she knew. "Adam lives up in a lovely valley on the back side of the mountains. There are only a few rough pine buildings there, however—a small general store, a stable and blacksmith shop; a building that serves as a community hall for circuit doctors and ministers and anyone doing something for the community. The community hall needs work, and that's one of our projects with the Missionary Society. We want to equip it with facilities for starting a school and church. I think Adam will be an important part of our dream."

Elisabeth nodded, considering her words. Everyone seemed to have a "part" in something. Star of the Morning had her mission in life; Adam had his. She had nothing—no identity, no family, nothing but a blank future staring her in the face.

"What's wrong, dear? You look troubled."

Elisabeth put her tea cup on the table and stood. "Actually, I'm pretty tired. It's been an adjustment learning my new job. I think I'll say good night now."

Mrs. Tillotson nodded. "Of course. Get a good night's rest. And, Elisabeth, I'd like you to accompany me to church on Sunday."

Elisabeth hesitated then nodded slowly. She had a real hunger to know more about the God who seemed to fill them with such goodness. She wished she were more like them.

"I'd like that," she replied. "Good night."

As soon as Elisabeth reached the quiet of her little room, the tears she had fought to keep back flooded forth, pouring down her cheeks. She sank onto the bed, burying her face in her hands. Her life seemed so empty and bleak, and she had never felt so lonely. Was God working in her life? Was He preparing her for some mission? Or would she have to live with this awful emptiness from now on?

twelve

Adam

The muscles of the big black horse rippled beneath his satinlike coat as he pulled the steep hill. Adam sat on his horse, gazing out across the snowy hillside, searching for animal tracks. He had seen some deer tracks, at least two day's old, but yesterday's winds had practically obliterated them. His eyes traveled upward to the bald eagle, soaring above a craggy peak. To Adam the eagle symbolized the wild, free beauty of Colorado.

He drew rein and sat back in the saddle. From his vantage point, he could see east to the dome of the mountain peaks, blanketed with fresh snow. His brown eyes returned to the valley below, to his rough, slab-pine cabin situated on a small plateau. Within that cabin, food was scarce, so he had taken up hunting. Some folks thought it was wrong to kill animals, but his father had told him early in life the Bible's teaching that man was to have dominion over the animals.

"But dominion is different from waste," his father reminded him. "We never kill an animal just for the sport of it. We only take an animal's life when we need food." As he thought of his father, a deep sadness welled in his heart. He needed to make peace with him, particularly now with the conflict raging between North and South.

The wind stirred through the pines, and Adam looked around, thinking maybe the deer would be bedding down. He had always felt a kinship with the animals, with all of nature. He believed this was due to his Cherokee background.

Suddenly Elisabeth Greenwood came into his thoughts. His prayer for her was that she would come to terms with her background, as he had. In his mind, the Ute heritage was a heritage to be proud of.

He dropped down from his horse, looped the reins around a pine trunk, and sat down on a dead log. A bitter wind howled down the mountain, ruffling his dark hair, but he didn't notice the weather now. He was consumed with thoughts of Elisabeth, and he didn't know how to deal with his feelings. It had been a week since his departure, and she had scarcely left his mind. He knew there could be no future for them until she found peace in her soul, and that meant turning to God for help. She would have to do this on her own; he had said all he was comfortable to say to her while she was still un-saved.

He hoped by now she had found a job. His funds were running low, as well. He would have to start panning the streams as soon as the snow started to melt. He had one nugget left, and that wouldn't take him far.

As he scanned the woods, he began to realize that tonight's meal would consist of more canned beans if he didn't ride the extra miles into the tiny trading post at Aspen Valley. He hadn't planned to go until tomorrow when he had been invited to the community hall to discuss the letter sent by the Denver Missionary Society. It was a dream come true that at last the group was raising money on behalf of Aspen Valley. So much was needed here. He would simply have to make two trips—one tonight and one tomorrow. He was hungry.

He pulled his six-foot frame upright again, shivering against the cold settling into his bones. The animals had dominion over *him* today. He would go to the post to spend his last nugget.

thirteen

The letter had been waiting for him at the post, and as he read it, it filled him with a combination of fear and dread.

> *Dear Adam,*
>
> *I hope this letter reaches you soon. The North and South are at war. I need you here to help me hold on to the land. Please come home.*
>
> *Your Father.*

Adam had spent a sleepless night, and by morning, he had decided to take a leave from his mission work to go south. He couldn't ignore his father's plea for help. He felt certain the mission board in Denver would understand.

As soon as his decision was made, he began to pack. He found his heart growing heavy, however, as he stood in the small cabin, looking around, thinking about leaving.

Sunshine spilled over the plain furnishings—the iron bed holding his bedroll, the wooden nightstand where a kerosene lamp sat beside his Bible. Pegs on the wall held his clothes. His eyes moved to the opposite end of the cabin, to the dining table and chairs with the three shelves on the wall containing his tin plate and cup and a few eating utensils, the woodstove that kept him warm and cooked his food.

Beside the small horsehair sofa sat another wooden table with a kerosene lamp and more books. It was a simple cabin, crude by city standards, and yet it had been home to him for two years. He hated to leave it.

He felt he had accomplished a lot, but there was so much more to be done. How long would his work be delayed?

The smell of mountain air and fresh pine filled his senses, and there was a bittersweet ache in his heart, knowing he might be leaving for good.

But there was no delaying what he must do.

fourteen

The trip into Denver seemed unusually long and tiring the next afternoon. He was weighted with the burden of resigning his ministry for a while, but he felt sure they would understand. And then he planned to drop by Mrs. Tillotson's to say good-bye to Elisabeth. It would not be easy, for he had thought of her often. She might be gone by the time he returned, or, considering how pretty she was and the inevitable suitors who would come calling, she could be married. That thought added to the heaviness growing in his heart.

❧

As they sat in Mrs. Tillotson's parlor, Elisabeth was strangely quiet.

"You really feel that you must go?" Elisabeth asked.

"I do. It's a matter of duty."

"But Tennessee is so far away." She looked across at him, her dark eyes troubled.

"Yes. I'm taking the night stage out. I've made arrangements with a friend here to keep my horse for a while. I'll write him about my future plans."

"Adam, will you write to me?" she asked, turning to jot down her address on a piece of paper.

"Yes, I'll write. It will help to make the time pass more quickly. And I would like for you to stay in touch," he added softly.

"I'll write you back," she said, handing him her address.

He nodded, glancing at her handwriting before folding the paper in half and inserting it into his pocket.

He looked down into her round dark eyes, wondering what she was thinking. Did she care for him? He wanted to believe she did. But he could not ask her to wait for him; that would be unfair. He forced himself to look away, to try to think about his departure and the task ahead of him once he reached home.

"I pray that you will be well," he said, glancing down at her again, for he could not keep his eyes from her face.

Her soft lips parted and their eyes locked. He took a deep breath and told himself there would be no good-bye kiss. It was difficult enough to say good-bye to her; he couldn't bear the thought of her kiss lingering in his memory, torturing him as their previous kiss had already.

"I will be fine," she said, lifting her chin proudly.

He nodded. "I'm sure you will. Well, good-bye."

He reached out, taking her slim fingers in his own for a moment and squeezing her hand gently. Again, he resisted the impulse to lean forward, touch his lips lightly to hers. No, it would only make matters worse.

Quickly, he released her hand, turned, and walked through the door, out into the cold winter night.

The stage seemed to jostle on forever, and to break up the monotony the trip, Adam decided to write to Elisabeth, as he had promised. He had purchased a tablet and pen at a stage stop the day before.

"Dear Elisabeth," his letter began. "The trip has been long and hard, but uneventful, thank God. There have been no raids on the stage by the Cheyenne or by army deserters who seem to be everywhere. Two other men rode with me, each returning to their home state because of the war. One was a Southerner from Mississippi, the other a Northerner from Pennsylvania. Strangely, we did not argue over the issues that started this war. There was a common bond among all of us to reach St. Louis safely."

He paused, staring out at the streets of St. Louis as they approached the next stage stop. There were Union soldiers everywhere, and he had already been told that Nathaniel Lyon had captured the Rebels in the city, taking them prisoner, and parading them through the streets of St. Louis. A small group of

Confederate sympathizers had rallied back in anger, starting a riot that resulted in more people being killed and wounded.

He returned to the letter, thinking ahead. "I am purchasing a horse and intend to start south today. Don't worry about me. I will remain safe, for I have no intention of letting anything stop my return to my father."

fifteen

Adam tried to push Elisabeth from his thoughts as he rode doggedly through the stormy spring night. He had never imagined he could miss someone so much, and yet her face was a sweet vision as he looked daily on the gaunt faces and disease-ridden bodies of the victims of war in Missouri and Kentucky.

He blinked his sleepy eyes and squinted into the dark night. There was only a pale quarter moon for light, and now that moon was obscured by wind-driven clouds. He blinked again and something scratched against his eyeball, a particle of dust from the back roads, which were a dense tangle of briars and vines.

His right cheek bore the slash of a sharp branch, and his clothes were clotted with debris and broken vines. Still, he preferred this to the gunfire of Yankee troops, or the Confederate army. Every day men out of uniform were being shot from their saddles as deserters. Neither army could bear the sight of a deserter, or even a strong, able-bodied man not fighting or impassioned with this war fever that bordered on insanity, it seemed to Adam.

He sighed. Judging from his last stop, he had one more hard day of riding before he would make it to his father's small farm in Tennessee.

As he shifted wearily in the saddle, his worn pants and shirt, washed out in creek water, scratched stiffly against his sore body. He now looked like a deserter, too. His beard, like the other men's, was thick and unkempt. His dark hair grew long on his neck beneath his battered felt hat.

Hearing a rustle in the dense woods behind him, he turned in the saddle. He saw the crack of fire a second before a sharp pain tore through his side. Toppling from his saddle, he lay facedown on the hard rough ground. Still and silent in total darkness, his assailant watched him.

He held his breath and lay motionless. The mold of decayed leaves and rain-soaked earth reeked in his nostrils, along with the sweat of his horse, nervously stamping the ground just behind him. At last he heard the cautious approach of another horse. Underneath him, his hand closed around a two-foot oak branch. His chest was nearly bursting from his indrawn breath.

The steps ceased. He heard the creak of the saddle as someone climbed down. Just as the boot of the assailant reached his side, he whirled over and swung the oak branch, knocking the soldier to the ground. Adam straddled the soldier, landing a hard right against his chin until the man slumped beneath him and lay still.

Peering through the semidarkness, Adam could see the Rebel uniform and the gaunt face of a boy, no more than sixteen.

"Oh, dear God," he moaned. "What has the world come to?" Sighing, Adam removed a strip of jerky from his pocket and shoved it in the boy's thin hand.

Turning, Adam pulled himself weakly onto his horse, hoping the clouds would slip away from the moon so he could see how badly he was wounded. Gently, he probed his own side as warm blood rushed over his hand. The bullet had penetrated just below the rib cage.

He yanked the ragged shirt from his back and ripped it up as best he could, then bound himself tightly, hoping to check the flow of blood. If he could slow the blood flow, maybe he could get to a farmhouse. As he turned his horse to plod slowly down the muddy road, he prayed.

God, help me. Send someone to help me. . .

For the first time since leaving Colorado, he doubted the wisdom of his long journey. He had underestimated the difficulty of escaping not only the soldiers, but worse, the deserters and thieves who prowled the night for money, horses, and food.

The night grew darker—or was he about to faint?

He squinted through the deep woods on both sides of the road, his ears strained, listening for the beat of horse hooves. Suddenly, an acrid smell floated through the trees, wafting beneath his nostrils, already filled with thick breath from his tightly squeezed chest.

He cocked his head and sniffed again. Smoke! Had the Yanks burned a farmhouse, or was he getting the drift of a campfire? He stopped his horse and turned his head from right to left, trying to identify the direction of the smoke. His senses drew him to the right, to the depths of the woods bordering the road. He had no idea how deep he must go into the woods to locate the source of the smoke or who might be at the campfire. But he had no choice. He would bleed to death if he didn't get help soon.

He slumped over the saddle, hanging on by sheer determination as his mind drifted in and out of consciousness.

The sticky blood filled his shirt bandage, and the whirling dizziness in his brain was worse than the vine-tangled path. He caught sight of a tiny patch of orange through the darkness and plunged on, finally coming upon a circle of men seated around a fire. The men wore gray uniforms. Two soldiers had bolted to their feet, their rifles drawn.

"Don't shoot," he gasped. "I'm a Southerner."

The curious faces faded from his vision, along with the glowing fire that promised warmth and perhaps food. He could feel himself slipping from the horse, and in those dark seconds, Elisabeth Greenwood's face swam through the darkness in his brain.

sixteen

A sharp pain seared Adam's side, a rotating pain that cut off his breath. His matted eyes dragged open, and he was looking into a lantern, then a bearded face above it.

"Lie still," the man commanded in a southern drawl. "Jim's digging the bullet out of your side. It may hurt a mite, but if he doesn't get it out, you're gonna die."

"Thanks," Adam rasped, unable to say more.

He gritted his teeth as the sharp gouging continued. He hadn't the strength to tell them who he was, to convince them he wasn't a deserter or a spy. He knew he must show courage, and he ground his teeth into his lower lip, determined to hold on. As the man said, he might die anyway. He might as well die with dignity.

He opened his eyes again and concentrated on the face above him. Bold blue eyes above a dark beard showed keen intelligence. Adam sensed the man was not a low-ranking officer, although he couldn't see the chevrons on his uniform. Dark brows slanted over his eyes, and the black hair beneath his Rebel cap was thick and curly. Adam had no choice but to trust the stranger, and as the pain swept over him, he gave in to a deep sleep.

so

A pleasant smell penetrated his senses. It occurred to Adam there was no pain now, and for a moment he lay reveling in the freedom from that torture.

Thank you, God.

A breeze rustling through the oaks picked up the drifting aroma, and his mouth began watering at the delicious scent. Slowly, he opened his eyes to a thin gray light. Dawn. In the distance, he could hear low voices, whispers. Again his stomach twisted with the pain of hunger, and he now understood why starving men ate whatever they could find.

He pushed himself up onto his left elbow, but the right side resisted, and he felt the stabbing pain again. His eyes dropped to his bare chest beneath the frayed blanket, and he saw a neat row of bandages covering his chest. He lifted his head and squinted at eight men seated around a morning fire. With surprise he noted the men were no longer wearing gray uniforms. Had he merely imagined that they were Confederate soldiers last night with his vision blurred and his mind desperate? They were dressed in old clothes, similar to the ones he wore. Suspicion and doubt warred within him, until he remembered they had saved his life. Whoever they were, they were his only friends right now.

"Morning," he called weakly.

The men whirled at the sound of his voice, and the blue-eyed man stood to his feet. He was not a tall man, nor was he muscled, but he moved with the agility of a forest animal, bounding quickly to Adam's side.

"We were wonderin' last night if you'd ever see daylight again. Who are you, and what happened?"

He swallowed against his dry, scratchy throat, hoping to speak clearly.

"I'm Adam Pearson," he answered. "I've been in Colorado for the past three years. I had started to Tennessee to check on my father." His voice was so weak that Adam wondered how convincing he must sound to these strangers.

A muscle twitched beneath the man's thick beard, and his blue eyes were now as cold as frozen seas. "You waited a long time to come home, mister."

Adam nodded. "Never thought of coming back, but after hearing stories of the war. . ."

"Well, I tell you what. . ." The man stroked his chin thoughtfully. "If you live, and I think you will, you can forget going any farther for a while. I doubt you'd get far alone. Anyway, you've just been drafted. I'm Captain Thomas Hines of the Ninth Kentucky. If you want to serve your country, you can start right now. We need you to help us push the

Yanks back."

When Adam considered his circumstances, he wondered if he really had a choice. He had already heard too many stories about deserters being shot by their own men, and while Captain Hines's tone was soft, Adam had seen the cold look in his eyes when Adam admitted he was not a member of the Confederate army.

He nodded slowly, as if in agreement, then closed his eyes again. A sadness engulfed him as his thoughts drifted back to Elisabeth. He prayed that no man had won her heart.

seventeen

Elisabeth

Winter finally dragged into spring while Elisabeth struggled to stay busy with her job. In the evenings, she and Mrs. Tillotson sat by the fire, discussing passages of Scripture. Elisabeth could feel her life changing ever since she began reading the Bible Mrs. Tillotson had given her. After attending church for the past month, Elisabeth had accepted Christ into her heart, and now her world was changing.

The bitterness she had felt toward Jed Greenwood was fading, along with the sharp ache of missing her mother. One thing had not changed, however; Elisabeth still missed Adam and longed to see him. She tried to keep up with what was going on in the South, but it was difficult. And the more she heard about the war raging, the more she worried about Adam. One evening as she sat by the fire with Mrs. Tillotson, she voiced her concerns.

"God will be with him," Mrs. Tillotson said, staring thoughtfully into the fire. "He's a fine young man. I pray every night that God will keep him safe."

Elisabeth swallowed hard. She had been praying that as well, but she didn't tell Mrs. Tillotson.

"I wonder when he'll come back," she said.

"I don't know, but when he returns I expect we will see him right away." Her eyes twinkled as she looked at Elisabeth.

"I hope so."

"I'm sure he will be calling on you."

"You're sure?" Elisabeth echoed, wondering what the little lady meant. It seemed to her Mrs. Tillotson knew a secret whenever Elisabeth asked her about Adam. She got a funny little smile on her face, and her eyes took on a mischievous twinkle.

"In case you hadn't noticed, Elisabeth, I believe Adam likes you."

Elisabeth's breath caught in her throat. "Why on earth do you say that?"

"A woman just gets a feeling about those things. And," she paused, giving her next words significance, "he asked me to take special care of you. I knew then he was smitten."

Elisabeth felt color rush to her cheeks. She was thrilled by those words, and yet she had thought Adam was just being a kind person who would have helped *anyone* in need. And she had certainly been in need. Still, Mrs. Tillotson's words were encouraging.

The next day after collecting her week's pay, she strolled into the mercantile and looked at the blue woolen dress again.

"Must have been meant for you," the salesclerk said. "There has to be a reason it hasn't sold before now."

Elisabeth stroked the nubby blue cloth, smiling with delight. "It *was* meant for me." She wished the same was true of Adam, but she tried not to let her hopes soar beyond reason as she took the dress home and hung it in her closet. This was her act of faith that she kept hearing about in church. She would not wear the dress until Adam came home, and then she would wear it for him.

❧

While war raged in the South, Colorado was torn with conflict between Indians, settlers, and outlaws. Several thousand men had left to enlist in the army while Civil War deserters and refugees flooded into the territory. It was a poor exchange, for the mines and gold mills fell to skeleton crews, while stealing and shoot-outs became commonplace in the streets of Pueblo, Colorado City, and Denver.

Elisabeth went straight to work and straight home each day, sometimes accompanied by Seth Wilkerson. She feared he was starting to see her as a possible wife, but she tried to maintain the proper balance between her business and personal life. Still, she was grateful for his concern. And still the blue dress hung in the closet, unworn, untouched, waiting for Adam's return.

eighteen

Adam and Elisabeth

As Adam healed, he tended the horses, kept a good campfire and cooked for the exhausted men. He had learned the reason the soldiers changed clothes as regularly as a company of traveling actors. They were a select group of General Morgan's men—Rebel Raiders, as they were known throughout Kentucky. Morgan had been a skilled calvaryman, but he excelled in more than calvary tactics. He was a master at conspiracy, a trait that seemed to distinguish the magnetic Hines, as well.

Adam had not challenged the men or argued with them about their beliefs. He did what he was told to do, but evenings by the campfire, he took his Bible out and read it. There were sneers on a few faces, but one by one, the soldiers came around night after night, asking questions about the Bible. After a particularly bad day, they seemed eager to have him share the Word of God, so they would have promises to cling to in battle.

This is hard, God, Adam prayed one night, as he lay awake staring through the warm darkness to stars twinkling overhead. *This is hard, but I know why you've placed me here.*

❧

Spring stretched to summer. Then, as Hines's troops pressed into Ohio and fought bravely at Buffington Island, they were finally captured. Adam, ill with fatigue and exhaustion, felt only a numb relief when his part in the raids ended.

The relief was short-lived, however, when the Confederate prisoners were loaded onto boats for a three-day journey to the prison at Cincinnati. As Adam huddled among the jostling bodies, the dull fog of exhaustion cleared from his mind, and the truth of his circumstances hit him with startling clarity.

His chances of reaching his father's farm in Tennessee had been slim before, but now they appeared impossible. His group was met by jeering mobs in Cincinnati who shouted taunts of "Hang them. . . hang them."

A guard shoved him into an overcrowded cell, and in the privacy of midnight darkness, Adam prayed desperately. Some of the men who had been talking with him about the Bible were now eager for anything he could tell them. Everyone feared they would die soon. While they were not permitted to talk with each other, some of the men used their utensils to communicate, carving words in food.

Bible verse?

Psalm 21, he wrote back. John 3:16. He had taught them about Jesus during their campfires, and had quoted the twenty-first psalm for one desperate, homesick young man. These soldiers seemed to remember everything he had told them, for sometimes he could see their mouths moving silently, and he would read the words on their lips. . . .

Should not perish but have everlasting life. . . .

On the third day in prison, the message Adam read in Hines's mashed potatoes brought hope to his heart. Hines had devised a means of escape—a tunnel to be dug under the dirt floor of the cell next to Adam's.

Adam knew it would take patience, determination, and a reckless disregard of the consequences to attempt the escape. But despite the obstacles, he felt that God was with them.

He moved his head in a cautious nod and Hines grinned. Adam knew in his heart that somehow he would make it to Tennessee.

nineteen

Elisabeth had taken to reading her new Bible nightly. After spending time in God's word, she would extinguish her lantern and pray earnestly for Adam.

"God, please bless him wherever he is. And please return him safely to us."

She also prayed that she could fulfill Adam's one request of her: accepting her heritage. The important thing was that God was her true heavenly Father. Each night as she crawled beneath the sheets of her bed and extinguished the lantern, she felt a calm assurance that He was going to work things out in her life. And in Adam's life as well.

❧

Adam's escape came in the wee hours, and to everyone's amazement, weeks of digging actually did pay off. The tunnel was tiny and cramped, but hope and desperation gave them the strength to force their bodies through to the far end where a patch of daylight waited. No good-byes were said; everyone fled into the dark night, hope in their hearts, a prayer on their lips.

❧

Elisabeth awoke in the middle of the night, her

heart racing, her forehead covered with perspiration. What was wrong? Something was wrong!

Her dark eyes flew over the room, assessing her situation. She was in her comfortable room at Mrs. Tillotson's house. All was quiet and still. She strained her ears. Had Mrs. Tillotson called out to her?

She leapt out of bed, peered through her open door to the hallway, where she could see across to Mrs Tillotson's room. The elderly lady preferred to have her drapes opened at night so she could lie in bed and look out at the stars.

Now the moonlight filtered through the lacy curtains, silhouetting Mrs. Tillotson, sleeping peacefully in her bed.

Elisabeth heaved a sigh. Thank God!

She stood for several minutes in the doorway, her ears straining, her eyes searching every darkened corner. Soon she convinced herself that nothing was wrong; all was just as it had been when she said good-night earlier.

Creeping back to bed and nestling under the quilt, the soft spring night flowed over her room, and she began to wonder about Adam. Was he in trouble? Had something happened to him? Had some inborn sense of alarm alerted her that he needed her prayers?

"Adam," she whispered into the darkness as new

pain wrenched her heart. Tossing the covers back, she knelt by her bed, her hands clasped together. And she began to pray for Adam, a prayer that went on for an hour.

twenty

Adam heard the words, and suddenly the world seemed to spin. When he reached out to grip the door frame for support, the woman's blue eyes were sympathetic.

"Sorry about your father, but he died peacefully in his sleep, I was told."

For a long time, Adam merely stared, scarcely able to believe that despite all he had gone through, he was still too late. Why had God allowed that to happen?

Tears glazed his eyes before he turned away. Before him, the rolling hills blurred through a haze of tears. He had always liked it here, but some part of his soul had never called it home.

He remembered his father's letter, asking him to come back and help him hang onto the land. He had failed.

"If it will make you feel better, he got your telegram," the woman said over his shoulder. "With the mail service paralyzed in places, it's a miracle word got through to him. But I found it among his possessions when we cleaned out the house. He knew you were coming home."

Those words were fresh inspiration to a man whose hopes were quickly dying in his heart. Adam turned back to face her, not caring that she saw his tears.

"Thank you. Who did you say you are?"

"We're the Canfields. My husband is a land speculator," she replied, "and we're from Washington. He bought up some of the land in this area by paying off the taxes. . . ."

Adam nodded, sick at heart.

"Where do you come from, young man?"

"Colorado," he replied, shoving his hands in his pockets. "And I'll be returning there."

"Did you travel through the country with war going on?"

He nodded, unable to say more. The past months were a nightmare for him. He had no idea how he was going to cross back through the same territory, particularly since he had escaped from a Yankee prison. Bitterness welled within him, but he fought back. He had to keep praying; he couldn't let hardship steal his faith.

"Listen, young man." The woman walked out to stand beside him. "It just so happens my husband is traveling with some men to St. Louis. You would be safe traveling that far with them. It's the least we can do for you. . . ."

He turned stunned eyes to her, scarcely able to believe what he was hearing. Just when doubt hovered like dark clouds, threatening to obscure all hope forever, here at last was a new ray of sun.

"I would be very grateful," he managed to reply. "I'm going to the family cemetery," he said. "And then I'll be back to talk with you."

"I'll have something for you to eat when you return," she said. Her eyes were filled with concern as she turned inside the house again.

"Thank you."

There was nothing left to do but visit his parents' grave and see for himself that they were gone. They were both Christians. Adam knew they were in a better place.

And still the tears streamed, unchecked, down his face as he swung into his saddle and turned his horse toward the family cemetery.

twenty-one

The return to Denver was surprisingly easy and without incident. With the help of Andrew Canfield, Adam reached St. Louis safely and was able to secure a horse and make his return to Colorado in less than a week. He had prayed throughout the journey that Elisabeth was still in Denver—and most of all, that she was not betrothed to another man.

❧

When Adam appeared at Mrs. Tillotson's front door, Elisabeth was there to meet him. As her eyes ran over him, her breath lodged in her throat. She could hardly believe that he was here. At home. Safe. At last.

He was a striking figure dressed in a dark broadcloth suit with a starched white shirt and gleaming black leather boots, gifts from the Denver Missionary Society upon his return home. His fashionable new round hat was dark, like his suit, and sat on his thick hair, trimmed neatly around his ears. His face was deeply bronzed from the winter wind and sun, accenting the vivid darkness of his eyes.

"Hello, Elisabeth," he said, removing his hat.

"Hello." She smiled up at him, delighted by the look of admiration on his face.

He had sent word that he would be arriving Friday afternoon and would like to see her. She was glad she had bought the dress.

"You look very pretty," he said.

"Thank you." She dropped her eyes to her hands, gripped tightly together before her.

Behind Elisabeth, Mrs. Tillotson cleared her throat and Adam looked in her direction.

"Good evening, Mrs. Tillotson. Would you like to accompany us to Apollo Hall? I've been told the play is a good one."

"Oh, no, thank you," she said on a little laugh. "At my age, the hearth is the best place for me on a winter night."

"Have you been well?" He smiled at her.

"I have. And you? We've prayed for you daily."

He hesitated for a moment. "I am well now. My father has passed away."

"Oh, I'm sorry." Elisabeth reached out, gripping his hand.

"Well," Mrs. Tillotson spoke up, "I want you to know that I've heard from the folks up in Aspen Valley. They're eager to have you back home. And your cabin is clean and waiting," Mrs. Tillotson informed him.

Adam shook his head. "How can I ever thank all of you?"

She waved the question aside. "Our thanks are to you. We decided not to replace you; you're irreplaceable. We're all excited that you'll be going back to the valley. Everyone up there sends you their regards. Now, you two have a good time," she said, letting her eyes drift back to Elisabeth as she stood waiting, her shawl on her arm.

"Here, allow me." Adam took her shawl and laid it lightly about her shoulders. "It's a warm night. I thought perhaps you would like to walk."

"That would be nice," Elisabeth replied, glancing back at Mrs. Tillotson. "I won't be late, Mrs. Tillotson."

Mrs. Tillotson merely waved and retreated back into her parlor as Adam and Elisabeth stepped out into the pleasant evening.

A soft golden twilight was settling over Denver as they strolled along, and Elisabeth felt a rush of happiness at just being with Adam. She turned to look at him, eager to relay her news.

"I have something to tell you," she said, looking up from the corner of her eye. She was still trying to adjust to her new ruffled bonnet, but having studied it in the looking glass from every angle, she decided it complimented her face. Watching Adam, she thought he must like it too, for he was smiling down at her with a huge grin on his face.

"What is it?" He reached for her gloved hand, inserting it into the crook of his arm.

"I became a Christian while you were away. Mrs. Tillotson gave me a Bible, and I'm reading it every night."

A wide smile lit his dark face. "Elisabeth, that's wonderful. How do you feel?"

"Much happier. And more at peace with myself."

He nodded thoughtfully, as his eyes trailed over her features. "You look different. I kept thinking it was because of your pretty clothes, but now I think it's the radiance from your soul."

He lifted her gloved hand to his lips and lightly kissed her fingers. "Elisabeth, I've missed you."

"And I've missed you, Adam," she said as their eyes locked. For a moment, they stopped walking until someone bumped into Adam at the street corner, drawing his attention back to their surroundings. "Well," he said, looking more serious, "we'd better hurry or we'll be late for the play."

❧

The play was performed by a troupe recently arrived in Denver. Elisabeth and Adam had joined a large audience to see *Richard III* acted out on a stage illuminated by candles, which added to the romance and intrigue of the story.

Afterward, Adam suggested a late supper at the

Tremont House, and they dined on hot tea and roast beef sandwiches. It was the first time Elisabeth had eaten in an elegant restaurant, and at first she was nervous about which fork to use or breaking the crystal glass or chipping the fine china. Adam soon put her mind at ease, however, as he began to talk about his work up in the mountains.

"Do you want to talk about the war?" she asked gently.

Adam stared at her, amazed that she was so sensitive to his feelings. "I'm not ready to talk about it yet. Maybe another time. I just want to enjoy being with you, and try to put these past miserable months behind me."

"Then that's what we'll do," she said, smiling into his eyes.

"Elisabeth," he said, then hesitated.

"What is it?"

He took a sip of tea. "Are you happy here?"

Her eyes drifted over the well-dressed crowd seated around them. "I should be. But there's an emptiness inside. Oh, it's much better since I became a Christian, but I want to do something more special with my life than working in the photography shop."

Adam leaned forward. "Do you have any ideas about what you'd like to do?"

She shrugged. "Maybe. I met Star of the Morning

this past year, and she's been back to visit a few times. She seemed so happy. . .so fulfilled."

"I know her," he nodded quickly, "and she is a wonderful young woman. The secret to that happiness, however, is her dedication to her work. To God's calling." He looked deeply into her eyes. "Would you want to do something like that?"

Elisabeth's breath caught in her throat. She sat very still, unsure how to respond. The conversation seemed to be getting very personal, and she wasn't yet sure how Adam felt about her. She felt reluctant to answer his question, but then she decided the best answer was an honest one.

"I still have to come to terms with my identity before I can make a success of anything." She toyed with her fork, wishing life did not always confuse her so much.

"Is it so important to you?" he asked.

She nodded quickly. "Yes, it is. Wouldn't you feel the same way if you were me?"

He took several seconds to consider her question then finally he responded slowly. "I suppose I would. In my case, I just always knew that I was part Cherokee, part white. I accepted it early, and it was never a problem."

"That's because you were loved," she said tightly.

His hand closed over hers. "Elisabeth, you are loved now. Can't that be enough?"

She stared at him, unable to believe her ears. Loved by Adam? Was it possible?

"I'm making you uncomfortable," he said, laying his napkin on the table. "Forgive me."

She wanted to tell him so much, to open up her soul to him, but for some reason she held back. Did he mean that *he* loved her? No, surely he was referring to Mrs. Tillotson, and maybe he meant that he loved her in the sense of brotherly Christian love. Something deep in her heart told her she was fighting with the truth, that the look in Adam's eyes was sincere. And yet, all the years listening to Jed Greenwood's rough voice, his constant belittling and scorning, had left her doubting that anyone could truly love her. Then when she returned to the post as practically an outcast. . .

"Shall we go?" Adam asked.

She hesitated, wanting to tell him how she felt, and yet the words were locked in her throat. She came to her feet, saying none of the things that filled her heart.

"When are you returning?" Elisabeth asked as they walked back to Mrs. Tillotson's house.

"On Sunday after services. Are you working tomorrow?"

She frowned. "I'm sorry to say that I am. Saturday has become our busiest day. But maybe you could stop by the shop," she suggested, turning hopeful eyes to him.

"I'll try to."

His tone was more reserved now, and she wondered if she had hurt his feelings by not responding. But they had been apart for months, and there was a deep sadness etched into Adam's face. She knew it was going to take time for him to heal from the war, and she wanted to be fair with him.

When they reached the doorstep, he lifted her hand to his lips, gently kissing her fingers. "I'll see you tomorrow," he said, almost as if he couldn't stay away.

The look in his eyes pulled at her soul, and she reached out to him, gently touching his cheek. "I hope so," she said.

He leaned down and kissed her, more passionately than before, and yet it was a brief kiss. And then he stepped back from her and she rushed inside, before she could have a chance to open her mouth and spill all the things at war in her soul out to him.

twenty-two

When she arrived at the shop the next day, Seth Wilkerson was standing in front of the *Gallery,* staring down the street, idly twirling his moustache.

"Good morning," she called.

"You're here," he whirled to her. "Good, I can leave." He grabbed his camera, slapped his round hat on his dark head, and almost ran over her. "I'm making pictures for the newspaper. Kit Carson has brought some Indians to town, and he's making a speech in a few minutes."

"Indians?" she repeated, following him out onto the sidewalk.

"Just some Utes," he tossed over his shoulder, hugging his camera under his arm and bounding down the board sidewalk.

Just some Utes. The words were like salt in an open wound, and she stared after him, startled by his indifference.

"Just some Utes?" she called after him, feeling an unexpected rush of temper.

She tilted her bonneted head back and gazed down

to the next street corner. At the corner of Larimer, a crowd was gathering around two men dressed in buckskins and leather, with long hair and beards, and dusty felt hats perched low on their heads.

Elisabeth stretched her neck, trying to see the object of everyone's interest. What if the Utes were from Lone Eagle's camp? What if this was someone she knew, one of the women who had been kind to her?

She felt herself being drawn toward the crowd, and she completely forgot her job and the *Gallery* as she inched toward the corner, peering around the onlookers.

Two ragged Ute children stood beside the men, one of whom was introducing himself as Kit Carson. He was rather short with bold features and keen eyes.

"The Utes and Arapahoes are at war," his voice rang out over the crowd.

Elisabeth searched the crowd for her employer; he was busily at work, focusing his camera. He wouldn't know she was anywhere in the background. She took a few steps closer.

"Last year when me and Jim Beckworth tried to persuade the tribes not to fight, we had no luck," Kit Carson's voice rang out. "Now, I'm askin' some of you to help these children. They were left without parents or a home, and the mission school is already overcrowded."

A hush fell over the crowd at first, then the silence turned into a flurry of whispers. No one stepped forward, however. Elisabeth bit her lip. Surely someone would help those poor children. . . .

Elisabeth was frozen with horror at the words Carson had spoken. Her mind raced back to Lone Eagle's camp. Were they being attacked by Arapahoes or white settlers? Compassion tugged at her heart, and she found herself wishing she could do something to help the children. Jed Greenwood had instilled a lifetime of prejudice into her thinking, but she could see now that it was wrong, all wrong.

"God forgive me," she silently prayed as she stared at the gaunt faces of the Ute boy and girl, the hollow dark eyes. They looked frightened to death. . .and hungry.

Without giving it another thought, she lifted her skirt and ran back to the bakery, yanking open the strings of her purse. She hadn't much money left, but she certainly had enough to buy a loaf of bread. And that was the least she could do.

By the time she returned with the warm bread wrapped in newspaper, most of the crowd had dispersed. Only a few curious ones still lingered at the edge of the street, staring at the children as though they were from a foreign land.

Elisabeth pushed past the people, oblivious even

to Seth Wilkerson, clicking his camera in the background.

"Here," she rushed up to the children, eagerly tearing the bread in half and giving each a generous piece.

The dark eyes were fearful as the children took the bread, while in the background she could hear someone whisper several words with one word more distinct: *Savages.*

She whirled on the man who had stumbled out from the saloon peering at the children with bleary eyes. "Savages," he called out, louder than before.

"They're not savages," Elisabeth yelled back at him. "They're human beings who deserve some respect."

Suddenly she realized how loudly she had spoken, and how quiet everyone had become. Then, in the blur of faces, she saw the red face of her employer and wasn't sure if the emotion on his face was sympathy or anger.

Giving the children one last smile, she turned and rushed back to the *Gallery* and dashed inside, slamming the door behind her. None of the people were more surprised by her reaction than she was. Removing her bonnet, she hung it on the peg by the door, while her thoughts lingered on the poor children. She couldn't forget their sad, tormented faces. Her stomach was comfortably filled with tea and oatmeal from Mrs. Tillotson's cozy kitchen. Her skin was covered with nice clothing, and yet those poor children were so in need. . . .

"Miss Greenwood," Seth Wilkerson burst through the door, "did you leave this shop unattended?"

She turned to him, still dazed by her thoughts. "What did you say?"

"I said. . ." He took a step closer to her, and she could see a hard glint in the dark eyes as he glared into her face. "Did you leave this shop unattended while you ran your goodwill mission? Obviously, you did. Do you have any idea how much of my money you risked by so carelessly wandering into the crowd?"

A frown marred Elisabeth's smooth brow as she struggled to make sense of his words. As she did, her eyes swept him up and down. He was as arrogant and uncaring as the drunkard she had yelled at.

"And you made quite a spectacle of yourself out there." His finger jabbed the air behind him. "It was an embarrassment to me."

"An embarrassment to you?" she cried out, horrified by his words. "Don't you even care that those children are cold and hungry? No, you don't," she said slowly, realizing for the first time what a self-centered little man he was.

"My concern is with my line of work and my business here in town, which you have just put at risk with your carelessness."

Elizabeth could feel her spine stiffen. "What do you consider most careless, Mr. Wilkerson?" she asked slowly, furiously. "Leaving your precious equipment unattended, which, by the way, nobody could work but you, and I'm not sure anyone wants to go around snapping that thing in people's faces." She pointed at his prize camera. "Or are you referring to my giving food to hungry children? Was that what you call making a spectacle of myself?"

"Boldly defending them against Tom Searcy, publicly embarrassing him?"

"The drunkard was doing perfectly well embarrassing himself. And he was drunk, in case you didn't notice."

"Tom Searcy spends a lot of money in this town. He's very successful in the trapping business. People don't yell at him."

Elisabeth took a step back from him, so furious she could hardly control the trembling that ran over her. And then a smooth deep voice spoke up in the background.

"And no one is going to yell at Miss Greenwood," the man said.

Elisabeth and Seth whirled simultaneously.

Adam stood in the door, glaring at Seth, his fists balled at his sides.

twenty-three

Elisabeth ran to his side, throwing her arms around him.

"Oh, Adam, it's all right." She turned back to Seth, who was boldly surveying Adam's fashionable broadcloth suit and round hat. "I'm not interested in working for you any longer."

She reached for her bonnet and cloak and linked her arm through Adam's. As soon as they were out the door, Adam gripped her hand and smiled down at her.

"I'm so proud of you," he said.

"For standing up to a mean little man?"

"And for defending the Indian children. I had just walked up to the *Gallery* to see you, when I spotted you on the edge of the crowd with the bread in your hand. I hurried down there and saw what you did. Before I could get to you, you had spoken your mind to the drunk and dashed off."

She looked at him sheepishly. "And you were proud of that?"

"Of course I was."

Elisabeth stopped walking and looked at Adam.

"Could we sit down and talk?"

"Of course."

They had reached a small park, and he led her to a bench where they took a seat. Elisabeth was oblivious to the people milling around as she looked into Adam's face and shook her head sadly.

"I've been so confused. But not anymore. Since I became a Christian and got my heart right with God, I feel as though the fog has cleared. It's been like a fog, you know. I was confused. . .lost. But you were right. My heavenly Father is the one who really matters."

"That's right," Adam acknowledged, "but still you must be at peace with your life and your past. How do you feel now about the Utes? Different, it seems."

"Different, yes. And ashamed for being so intolerant, so prejudiced. If I am half Ute, these are my people who are being treated like animals, Adam."

He nodded and sighed, turning her gloved hand over in his and staring at it. "Many years ago, I felt the way you're feeling now. I knew I had to stand for something, to help those who were being mistreated. I've never regretted my decision."

She tilted her head back and looked at him. "Maybe that's what I'd like to do."

"Nothing would make me happier," he said, pulling her into his arms as they both ignored the stares of people around them. He hugged her against his chest, and neither spoke for several seconds. Then he gently pushed back from her and looked down into her eyes. "I want you to think and pray about that decision. And if you still mean it, when I come back to town, I want to take you home with me."

"Home with you?" she gasped.

"As my wife. It won't be an easy life, Elisabeth. I travel a lot, and you would be left alone in the cabin. Well, not alone," he chuckled, "because I'm always taking in strays who need help."

"I wouldn't mind," she said softly, gazing up into his eyes.

For several seconds neither spoke. Then Adam stood and pulled her to her feet. "We mustn't do anything hasty. You think about this, and I will too."

"I won't change my mind," she said softly as they walked back to Mrs. Tillotson's house.

"Just be sure. And to be fair about it, you need to come up to the valley and see what my life is like. Maybe we can persuade Mrs. Tillotson to accompany you."

She shook her head. "She won't travel until spring."

"Then I'll think of something," he said, leaning down to kiss her cheek.

"Maybe you should just take me home with you now. As your bride."

He stopped walking, staring down into her eyes, unable to believe his ears. "Are you sure about that?" he said, his voice choked with emotion.

"I've never been so sure of anything in my life!" she said and began to laugh.

It was true—all that mattered to her was being with Adam and serving God wherever He sent them.

Adam began to laugh with her as they quickened their pace back to Mrs. Tillotson's house.

"Mrs. Tillotson is going to be surprised," Elisabeth said, as he hugged her tightly.

"I don't think so. I told her the day I brought you to her house that I might come back and marry you someday."

She whirled to stare at him. "How did you know that?"

"I didn't. I just asked God to work things out and He did."

Tears filled her eyes as she looked at Adam and smiled. "Yes, He worked things out just perfectly."

A Letter To Our Readers

Dear Reader:

In order that we might better contribute to your reading enjoyment, we would appreciate your taking a few minutes to respond to the following questions. When completed, please return to the following:

Rebecca Germany, Managing Editor
Heartsong Presents
P.O. Box 719
Uhrichsville, Ohio 44683

1. Did you enjoy reading *Song of the Dove?*
   ❑ Very much. I would like to see more books by this author!
   ❑ Moderately
   I would have enjoyed it more if _____

   _____

2. Are you a member of **Heartsong Presents**? ❑Yes ❑No
   If no, where did you purchase this book? _____

   _____

3. What influenced your decision to purchase this book? (Check those that apply.)

   ❑ Cover   ❑ Back cover copy

   ❑ Title   ❑ Friends

   ❑ Publicity   ❑ Other_____

4. How would you rate, on a scale from 1 (poor) to 5 (superior), the cover design? _____

5. On a scale from 1 (poor) to 10 (superior), please rate the following elements.

    ___Heroine   ___Plot

    ___Hero   ___Inspirational theme

    ___Setting   ___Secondary characters

6. What settings would you like to see covered in **Heartsong Presents** books?_____

_____

_____

7. What are some inspirational themes you would like to see treated in future books?_____

_____

_____

8. Would you be interested in reading other **Heartsong Presents** titles?   ❏ Yes   ❏ No

9. Please check your age range:
    ❏ Under 18   ❏ 18-24   ❏ 25-34
    ❏ 35-45   ❏ 46-55   ❏ Over 55

10. How many hours per week do you read? _____

Name _____

Occupation _____

Address _____

City_____ State_____ Zip _____

·········· Presents ··········

Great Inspirational Romance at a Great Price!

Heartsong Presents books are inspirational romances in contemporary and historical settings, designed to give you an enjoyable, spirit-lifting reading experience. You can choose wonderfully written titles from some of today's best authors like Peggy Darty, Tracie J. Peterson, Colleen L. Reece, Lauraine Snelling, and many others.

When ordering quantities less than twelve, above titles are $2.95 each.